"You're officially reneging on your proposal?"

Falcon nodded. "Yes, ma'am."

"All right." Taylor took a deep breath and stepped close to him. She poked a finger in his chest, and he'd never wanted to grab her and kiss her senseless as badly as he did at that moment. "Listen to me, you big chicken. I wouldn't marry you if you were the last man on earth."

Thankfully she hadn't come to tell him she'd picked another bachelor and was ducking out of the so-called agreement. That had been his greatest fear when she'd pulled up in the Jeep. The relief was practically blinding.

"Okay," he said, smelling her sweet perfume. "I accept that."

"You will accept it, because I'm not giving you a choice." Her eyes flashed at him. "I'm having a baby, and the last thing I'd ever do is to marry a chickenhearted weasel who's scared to death of his own feelings."

Falcon felt as if a boulder from the canyons had fallen on him, crushing him. He could barely breathe. "A baby? My baby?"

Dear Reader,

The Callahans love their family, their land and the Diablo mustangs that run free through the New Mexico canyons. In this newest chapter of the Callahan legend, Falcon Chacon Callahan has had his eye on Taylor Waters for a long time, but the independent brunette isn't exactly the kind of woman who's ready to make a run to the altar. Taylor likes the rangy, sexy cowboy, but everyone knows that Falcon—like all the Callahans—is wild at heart. Will their love unite them against the evil forces swirling around Rancho Diablo? Or are Taylor and Falcon destined to be the first who elude Aunt Fiona's matchmaking magic?

As the first warmth of spring begins to tease us from our winter hibernation, I hope you will enjoy riding the range with Taylor and Falcon. The lore of the Diablo mustangs is a rich part of the tapestry of Rancho Diablo, and it's my greatest wish that you enjoy discovering the mystical call of their spirits with these hard-loving cowboys.

Much love,

Tina

www.tinaleonard.com

www.facebook.com/tinaleonardbooks

His Callahan Bride's Baby

TINA LEONARD

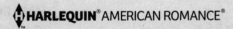
HARLEQUIN® AMERICAN ROMANCE®

Recycling programs
for this product may
not exist in your area.

ISBN-13: 978-0-373-75449-6

HIS CALLAHAN BRIDE'S BABY

Copyright © 2013 by Tina Leonard

Printed in U.S.A.

ABOUT THE AUTHOR

Tina Leonard is a *USA TODAY* bestselling and award-winning author of more than fifty projects, including several popular miniseries for Harlequin American Romance. Known for bad-boy heroes and smart, adventurous heroines, her books have made the *USA TODAY*, Waldenbooks, Ingram and Nielsen BookScan bestseller lists. Born on a military base, Tina lived in many states before eventually marrying the boy who did her crayon printing for her in the first grade. You can visit her at www.tinaleonard.com, at www.facebook.com/tinaleonardbooks and www.twitter.com/tina_leonard.

Books by Tina Leonard

HARLEQUIN AMERICAN ROMANCE

Best wishes to Kathleen Scheibling and Roberta Brown for believing in the Callahan series, and also to my children, Lisa and Dean, who are my own personal dream. Last though never least, my best wishes to the wonderful readers who have supported my writing and my dreams for so many years. Thank you to each and every one of you for being the most kind and dedicated readers on the planet.

Chapter One

"The thing about the Callahans is that if they call you friend, there's nothing they won't do for you. But woe if they call you enemy."
—Bode Jenkins, talking to a reporter

Rumor had it that Taylor Waters was one of Diablo's "best" girls. She had a reputation for being wild at heart. Untamable. Men threw their hearts at her feet.

She walked on those hearts with a sweet-natured smile, and guys ate it up with a spoon.

Falcon Chacon Callahan studied the well-built brunette in Banger's Bait and Tackle. He'd talked the owner of the diner, Jillian, into selling him one last beer, even though the diner usually closed at the stroke of midnight on weekends. It was his Saturday night and he hadn't wanted to do anything but relax and consider what he was going to do with his life once his job at Rancho Diablo was over.

Taylor was a more immediate interest. She smiled that cute pixie smile at him, and Falcon sipped his beer, deciding on a whim—some might call it a hunch—to toss his heart into the Taylor-tizzy. Intuition had been known to save his life on several occasions, so Falcon believed in living by his spontaneous side. "I need a wife," he said, and she grinned.

"So I hear. So we all hear." She came and sat on the bar stool next to him. "You'll get it figured out eventually, Falcon."

Taylor worked hard to support herself and to help out her sick mother. There was no Pop Waters anymore, just mother and daughter trying to manage things on their own. Falcon understood how tough it was to be without a parent. "Marry me, Taylor."

"I've only served you three beers and a plate of fajitas. I know you're not drunk enough to propose, Falcon. You're just crazy, as everyone in Diablo already knows." She smiled so adorably all the sting fled her words. In fact, she was so cute that Falcon felt his chest expand with admiration.

"I leave crazy to my brothers. My sister is the nutty one. Me, I'm somewhere on the other side of the spectrum." He leaned over and kissed Taylor lightly on the lips, not caring anymore that he had spent much of his life avoiding the marriage trap. To win the land north of Rancho Diablo, across the deep, winding canyons, he had to have a wife and family. Taylor would do just fine. She packed a generous fanny, and he thought that boded well for childbearing. She also had a nice rack, and that boded well for him.

He grinned. "What's your answer, cupcake?"

"You're not serious." Taylor shook her head. "I've known you for over a year. Of all the Callahans, you're the one the town's got odds on being last to the altar." She got up, sashaying to the register. His eyes followed her movements hungrily. "A girl would be a fool to fall for you, Falcon Callahan."

That did not sound like a yes.

"Aren't women supposed to be happy to do all that wedding stuff? Trust me, my offer's good as solid gold."

She laughed. "Jillian, Falcon wants to marry me."

Jillian barely glanced up. "Don't do it, honey," she said. "No need for you to marry down."

"Wait a minute," Falcon said, sitting up straighter. "Marrying down is just as honorable as marrying up. Don't tell her to pass on a rascal on principle, Mrs. Banger." He looked at Taylor. "Good advice isn't something you want to take every time, sugar."

"Oh, goodness." Jillian finally gave up on the receipts she'd been studying. "Falcon, why in the world would Taylor want a wild man like you?"

He smiled. "I didn't say it was a good deal for her. It would be a good deal for me."

"That's not the way marriage works." Taylor lightly tossed a dish towel at him as he got up from the bar stool. "It's supposed to be good for both parties."

"Some things would be very good. You would not lack for the things ladies *really* like." He noted Taylor's blush with a satisfied smirk. "I could convince you to like me if you give me a chance, Taylor. Just think about it. I'm offering you a helluva good time."

"How could I ever pass an offer like that up?"

He grinned at her freckle-sprinkled nose and sexy, full lips. "Modestly as I can say it, you shouldn't."

"Let me butt in," Jillian said. "Here's what I think, Falcon. This is August. If by Christmas you're still interested, you can ask Taylor again—after you've got your act together. It's only about three and a half months. The best things are worth waiting on." She said it kindly, but very seriously, and Falcon knew that Taylor was taking Jillian's words under advisement. The little brunette was studying her boss as if Jillian was some kind of oracle.

Or fairy godmother.

Interfering fairy godmothers could be a bad thing. He knew this from experience. His spry and determined aunt Fiona occasionally tried to play at good-natured manipulation of people's lives, with mixed and sometimes disastrous results.

Falcon sighed. "I really didn't want to have to work hard for a bride, Mrs. Banger. I wanted this to be an easy thing."

Taylor raised a brow. "Whoever told you I was easy?"

He put up a soothing hand before female hackles rose. "I never said that. I said I wanted an easy marriage. Maybe even a quick baby. I leave that part up to you."

"And then?" Taylor asked.

"Hell, I don't even know what's going to happen tomorrow," Falcon said honestly. "I guess if we could stand the sight of each other after nine months of baby-making, we'd still sit on the porch together."

"You're not serious." Taylor laughed. "Why don't you just order a bride? Or meet a woman on one of those internet sites?"

"Because," Falcon said, considering her sweet lips and friendly face, "I might not like her the way I like you."

"You don't like me," Taylor said. "You've been coming in here for months, and you've never asked me out. Never did more than sit here and eat fajitas and drink a beer or two."

"A guy just doesn't blurt out that he thinks a girl's

got a fine butt and a nice, uh, smile, the first time he comes into her diner. I was working up to it."

He paid his tab, realized he hadn't completely made his case. "So what happens in December, Mrs. Banger?"

"Oh, a lot happens *before* December," Jillian said. "I'm going to fix Taylor up with every eligible man I know, and every bachelor the ladies of the Books'n'Bingo Society know, and I'm sure Taylor's aunt, Nadine Waters, knows quite a few. And then if Taylor wants to marry you come December, then I guess I won't be able to stop her." She smiled. "They say nothing gets in the way of true love, Falcon."

He put his hat on. "Yes, ma'am." He went over and kissed her on her cheek, as he always did. "I'm going to live up to your expectations. You just wait and see." He glanced at Taylor, who leaned up against the bar, her arms crossed, watching him. "You pick out your wedding gown. A Christmas wedding will work fine for me."

"Good night, Falcon."

That was all she said. It was enough. Jillian could fix Taylor up with all the men she liked, but in the end, Taylor was going to choose him.

He would see to that. Nobody had said romance and lovemaking were off the list—just no marriage proposal—and he did his best convincing in the sheets.

Those terms suited him just fine.

Falcon's brothers, along with their sister, Ashlyn, were sitting in the upstairs library of Rancho Diablo when he walked in the next night. As he headed over to fix himself a whiskey before the weekly meeting, an explosion of colored confetti showered down on him. His siblings roared with laughter.

"What the heck's going on?" Falcon demanded.

"We heard about your marriage proposal, brother dear," Ash said. "We wanted to celebrate your effort, paltry though it was."

"Thanks." He flung himself onto a leather sofa. "How did you hear?"

"Word travels fast on Diablo's grapevine." His eldest brother, Galen, wore a grin on his pumpkin head that was positively gleeful.

The twins, Tighe and Dante, shook their heads. He had no comment for them. They'd been chasing two nannies—bodyguards in disguise—and that had gone nowhere fast for either of them. River and Ana seemed completely immune to what his brothers had to offer, and that was a great source of amusement to the Callahan clan. "Shut up," Falcon said to Tighe and Dante, who snickered.

"We're happy for you," Ash said. "You made an effort. It's progress. Even if you proposed in a diner. Couldn't you have classed it up a little? We have a family reputation to uphold. We may be spontaneous, but we're always classy."

"Jeez." Falcon examined his glass before he emptied it. "She didn't say yes. Yet."

"What made you decide to ask Taylor Waters to marry you?" Jace asked. "She's a hot little thing, sure, but you'll never get her, you know. She's out of your league. Smarter than you. Nicer, too."

It was no surprise to Falcon that Jace couldn't understand. Jace was an earth lover, a man of his heritage, and he was young. He was the only one of the siblings who actually wanted to settle down. Jace dreamed of a wife and family.

Falcon had had to sneak up on the idea of marriage a bit more slowly. First, he hadn't met that many women. He worked a lot, like everyone else in this room. They were soldiers, all of them, trained for covert ops and sniper fire, and everything else one faced in the Special Forces. The job wasn't the best backdrop for casual dating. Anyway, the first time he'd laid eyes on Taylor, something had hit him in the gut. And it had hurt so good he'd known he was onto something with the spicy brunette.

"Sloan, you're settled now, got kids," he said. "What do you think about marriage?"

Sloan smiled. "I recommend it. Just maybe not with the first girl you lay eyes on. It's all fine and good to try to win the ranch land, but maybe you don't want to propose every day that ends in *y* until you finally pick off a female. Be patient. Eventually a woman will take pity on you."

"Very funny." Falcon grimaced. "It can't be that hard. Marriage is just a contract between two people."

Ash came over to sit next to him, leaned against his shoulder. "You really want that land, don't you?"

"Look who's talking—you've already named it," he pointed out. "I've got a name chosen for when I win it, too."

Galen sighed. "This is what Aunt Fiona and Running Bear want, all of us focused on the land and settling down at the drop of a hat. They did it to our Callahan cousins, and they're going to be really happy to see all of us sink like rocks into the wedding swamp."

"Swamp?" Dante laughed. "Even I wouldn't have

thought of Aunt Fiona's wedding dare as a swamp. Maybe a soup."

His twin, Tighe, shuddered. "Swamp works for me."

Jace got up, went to look out a window. "I'm looking as hard as I can for a bride. It's not happening."

"They say a watched pot never boils," Sloan said. "Maybe your fire's not turned on."

"My fire's fine," Jace snapped. "Let's not worry about my fire, thanks."

"I move we get on to the general business." Falcon felt edgy, impatient. "Any news?"

"Fiona mentioned the chief dropped by." Galen's expression turned intense. "She said Running Bear wants to meet with us tonight in the stone circle."

"Did our cagey aunt say what the topic is?" Falcon asked.

Ashlyn smiled, her once-short, light blond hair now grown just past her ears, making her look less soldier these days and a bit more delicate. "Apparently, Running Bear may have word about our parents."

Falcon blinked. They hadn't heard from their parents in years. At least twelve. He tried to remember. He was thirty-three now—he'd last seen their parents...on his twenty-first birthday.

Ash, the baby, had been thirteen, Dante and Tighe fifteen.

Falcon had been a man then—but it hadn't felt like it. Galen had come home from his medical studies in the military to keep them in line. The siblings had tested Galen, giving him a bit of hell, but it hadn't lasted long. Those who were of age followed him into the military. The rest Galen ramrodded into growing up good.

Good and tough.

He looked around at his siblings. "Well, that would be news. If it were true."

They all gazed at him. He sighed.

"I'm sorry. I can't get excited about it. It's been too many years and too many dead ends in the maze." He shrugged. "We all know how the story ends, anyway."

They looked away. Falcon knew his words were perhaps harsh, but they were honest. He went to the windows and stared out at the vast horizon toward the canyons, feeling angry, hurt, somehow betrayed, even though he knew their parents had done exactly what he would have done—and would do, at this very moment if necessary, to protect his family.

He didn't focus on the pain anymore. It didn't do any good. He held his parents' memories inside him, respecting them, knowing they were in his heart, where they could never be taken away from him.

Still, peace was elusive.

There was not going to be a happy reunion, and he knew it as well as the rest of his family did.

He brooded about that—until he saw shadows swirling in the evening light washing the distant mesas. "Look," he told his brothers and sister, and they came to stand beside him. They watched as the mystical Diablos, a sure portent of things to come, thundered through the painted canyons.

Yes, he would make the very same decision his parents had made. It was all about protecting the family—and right now, his mission was guarding his parents, Callahan cousins, Rancho Diablo, and the Diablos from the danger stalking them.

JILLIAN LOOKED AT TAYLOR as she finished tidying up the diner's mahogany counter. "You don't want him to know, do you?"

Taylor didn't look at her old friend and employer. "Falcon isn't serious about marrying me. He doesn't need to know anything about my private life."

"He sounded pretty serious to me." Jillian cocked her red mop of hair, thinking. "Callahan men usually stick to that 'strong, silent type' way of thinking, but say what's really on their mind." She nodded. "Maybe you should tell him the truth."

"Falcon doesn't need to know that I received another marriage proposal. It's none of his business." At the moment, Taylor didn't want anyone in Diablo to know more about her than necessary. She'd grown up here. People talked, and talked *a lot*. And she hadn't quite accepted the astonishing proposal of Storm Cash. She'd said she'd think about it.

Falcon's proposal was the second she'd received in a month. "I'm in shock, to be honest."

"I am, too." Jillian walked over, took the dishrag from her. "Go home. Think about all this. Talk to your mom about everything. It's not often a woman gets proposals from two men almost at the same time."

"They're enemies," Taylor murmured.

"True enough." Jillian nodded. "Falcon's going to hear about it eventually."

A chill teased at Taylor. "Do you think he knew that Storm proposed?"

"I feel certain that Falcon isn't the kind of man to do things out of a sense of competition for a female. There's too many pretty ladies around who would give anything to go out with him, or any of the Callahan boys." She shrugged. "Tell me again why Mr. Cash offered to marry you?"

"He said he needed a wife," Taylor said. "He said he'd heard that Mama was ill, and he didn't want to take me away from her when he knew she needed help, so he would wait for me. But he also wanted to help Mama out. I told him we were fine, that we didn't need his assistance. To be honest, I thought his proposal was more sincere than Falcon's."

"Never underestimate a Callahan. They don't do anything half-baked. It just seems like they're half-baked, all of them." Jillian laughed. "They are wild men, for sure—both sides of the Callahan family tree. And Ash follows in her brothers' and cousins' footsteps. In fact, I do believe Ash taught those boys a thing or two about staying crazy and free, at least according to what Fiona has shared." She smiled, enjoying telling the yarn. "No, Callahans are fully baked, like clay fired in a kiln. Falcon was serious."

Taylor realized she'd completely dismissed Storm's proposal, kind as it might have been. Yet her heart had leaped at Falcon's words—first in surprise, then with what she could only identify as happiness, even as she knew he couldn't truly love her. He was too wild.

How long had she carried a secret torch for the handsome, long-haired cowboy? Months. Maybe ever since he'd ridden into Diablo. She heard the tales of wildness surrounding him and his family, and every time he'd come into the diner and ordered a meal, his dark navy eyes staring into hers, her heart had sung.

"You better straighten it out, honey, if you've got a yen for that man." Jillian turned the lights low and switched on the small neon closed sign in the window.

"I can only warn you that if you have any feelings at all for Falcon, any idea at all that you might want to consider dating him, you want to turn down Storm Cash as quickly and quietly as possible. If Storm should tell anyone in Diablo that he offered to marry you, Falcon will run in the opposite direction. Those two are natural enemies, like an alpha wolf crossing into another alpha's territory. You have to decide if you want either of those gentlemen, or neither, before they catch wind of each other. Some men compete over a girl, but I think Falcon's got too much baggage and too many girls after him to expend the effort. He did say he was looking for an easy thing." Jillian gently smiled. "I wish I was still young enough to have two sexy hunks vying for my hand in marriage."

Taylor picked up her purse and followed Jillian from the diner. It was hot now in New Mexico. There were fires burning in different parts of the state, feeding on the parched land. Soon, hopefully, the heat would break, and more temperate conditions would settle over Diablo.

Christmas wasn't that far away.

"You could get him if you play your cards right," Jillian said cheerfully. "And if you want to know about playing man cards, you might consider asking his aunt for information. Goodness knows no one loves a wedding like Fiona Callahan."

Once again, Taylor felt that leap in her heart.

And guarded herself against it.

Chapter Two

"Don't know if you've heard," Ash whispered in Falcon's ear as they crouched around the white stone circle near the canyons that night, "your sweetie's in town agitating."

He couldn't help a smile at the thought of Taylor "agitating." She was a firecracker, and he was dying to light her on sexy fire. "What's up?"

Ash seated herself cross-legged on the ground and grinned. "First, it seems she has a problem with the way one of her neighbors is treating his horses. Taylor's been making noise about someone needing to take the animals from their owner. Then," Ash continued, as if that wasn't enough for one woman to tackle, "Taylor's decided the town elders need to do something about the panty raid the high school kids had on Friday night. Some people thought it was harmless fun, but some people thought the kids ought to get suspended, since all the panties ended up on the lawn of Miss Lyda's old folks home south of town." His sister laughed, delighted.

Truthfully, he didn't care much about the shenanigans of the high schoolers, and preferred to spend some time thinking about the type of panties Taylor might wear. "What's Taylor agitating for?"

Ash grinned. "She thinks the high schoolers involved need to be commissioned for a sing-in on the porch of Miss Lyda's, to entertain the live-in residents. And she wants them to spend an afternoon painting Miss Lyda's fence and porch to freshen it up a bit. Miss Lydia does her best, but everybody's wallets are a little thinner these days. She could use the help. Taylor believes the kids need to spend a little time around their elders, who could teach them a thing or two about life. Panty raids are fun, she told the town council, but life lessons are important, too."

And that's why Diablo loved her. Falcon grunted. "If she gets it arranged, I'll put up the paint."

"You will?" Ash stared at him.

"Yeah." He shrugged. "The town's wallet isn't so full these days, either. And I'll go check out the farmer whose horses Taylor thinks aren't in great shape."

"Why are you doing this?" Ash demanded. "I mean, I guess it's obvious, but it's not necessary, just because you lost your mind for a moment and proposed. You don't have to convince her you're a saint."

"I'm no saint." That was absolutely true. Falcon couldn't care less if people thought he was saint or devil. "I need to get off my butt, anyway."

"Yeah. Right." Ash gave him a sidelong look. "We prefer to keep your goodness under wraps, you know. Your Boy Scout side is for family consumption only. You're going to make Taylor fall in love with you."

"That's the plan."

Ash shook her head. "I'm beginning to think you honestly mean that."

Taylor was strong, strong enough to match him and

stand up to him. She wouldn't wither away under the stress of his lifestyle.

Their grandfather came to the circle and lit the small fire.

"You remember that you were brought here to protect Rancho Diablo, the Diablo spirit mustangs and your cousins," Running Bear said. "The Callahan bond to earth and sky is strong."

His brothers and Ash nodded. Falcon stayed still, his gaze on his grandfather's weathered face.

"More importantly, you know that you protect your parents, Julia and Carlos, and the parents of your Callahan cousins, Jeremiah and Molly, from discovery. From attack. Dark forces have gathered on the land in the canyons and gorges. In the last year, three mercenaries have followed your every move, even kidnapping one of your women."

Falcon glanced at his brother Sloan. Sloan's wife, Kendall, had been briefly kidnapped by one of the mercenaries, who'd turned out to be a family relative—Uncle Wolf, brother to Jeremiah and Carlos, and determined to harm his own brothers. Wolf was the dark, fallen angel of the family.

"Now that the Diablo Callahans remain in Hell's Colony, Texas, it should have become quiet here at Rancho Diablo." Running Bear looked at the sky for a moment, thoughtful. "You will be stretched a little thin when Dante and Tighe leave."

Falcon stared at his brothers. The twins looked a bit sheepish in the face of their family's shock.

"What do you mean?" Ash demanded. "Where are you going?"

"We might try our hand at rodeo," Dante said. "We're

not cut out for this detail. The constant waiting is making us crazy."

"Yeah," Tighe said. "It's like we're waiting for a war that never starts."

"Finks," Ash told her brothers. "How can you turn your backs on family? Jonas and Aunt Fiona and Uncle Burke wouldn't turn their backs on you!"

Dante and Tighe looked crestfallen at their sister's criticism.

"Let them go," Running Bear said. "Dreams cannot be ignored. They must be lived."

"Oh, bother." Ash glared at her brothers. "Well, maybe I'll go off on a toot myself. Maybe we'll all just pack up and go off chasing rainbows and unicorns."

"You can't," Dante said. "Who would watch over Fiona?"

"It's all right," Falcon said, opting to play the role of peacemaker. "The ranch will survive."

Ash turned her head away from Dante and Tighe. Falcon thought his brothers seemed to shrink at her obvious censure of them.

"I agree with Falcon," Galen said. "We're all following our own dreams. We have to live our lives to some extent. This commission is going to take years. Besides, Falcon's proposed to a woman in town. Sloan's married. Life goes on."

"We just don't feel like we're doing anything," Tighe said. "The mercenaries haven't been around in months. For all we know, they're gone."

They all looked at Running Bear. He shrugged. "Tonight, you must focus on deciding to stay here or to go. This ring of stone and fire is your home, for as long as you want it to be."

"We're never going back to the tribe, are we?" Jace asked.

Running Bear shook his head. "That path would lead the enemy to your parents' door. I remind you that one of you is the hunted one. You must guard against any division that may reside inside you. There will come a time when you have a split second to make a decision, a moment when you stand at a fork in the road. You will not recognize the danger, but the choice you make will live with you, and all of us, forever. Until then, here you stay, until you walk away."

His grandfather's ominous words were chosen carefully, a warning. Falcon had only one choice, and that was to stand and fight. "I'm staying. Rancho Diablo's good as anyplace else to live, and besides, I really like Aunt Fiona and Burke." For that matter, he liked the town of Diablo. He felt his soul take flight on the rare occasion when the Diablos were spotted in the dusty canyons that were the ancient, stunning backdrop to the ranch. "Family's first with me. I'm a soldier, and then I'm a family man. Can't walk away from a good fight, especially since it involves family." He tossed a handful of dirt into the fire, where it briefly dimmed the flames.

"I'm staying," Ash said. "I'm hard core." She flung dirt into the fire and walked to kiss her grandfather on the cheek, then mounted her horse. "I've got land to win," she told her brothers. "The only way to win is to hang tough."

"And lure Xav Phillips to fall for you," Dante said.

"Good luck with that," Tighe said.

"Just because you two got dumped on your heads by the nanny bodyguards is no reason to doubt Ash," Falcon said. "She's smarter than all of us. Good luck with the rodeo. Let us know where you're riding sometime. We might come around."

He left the stone circle, following his sister off on horseback. He knew who would stay and who would go; there was no need to linger.

Every man had to do what he had to do.

Falcon was called to serve.

FALCON KEPT FOLLOWING Ash the second he realized his sister wasn't heading toward the Tudor-style Rancho Diablo mansion with the seven chimneys, but toward the canyons. He knew Xav practically lived in the canyons, rarely returning to the ranch for supplies, but Ash wasn't heading in the right direction. It looked as if she was skirting the deep crevasses of the mesas, heading to the opposite side of where Xav kept his camp.

Falcon tried to envision what life would be like if he didn't have a headstrong sister, and realized it would be dull as dirt. Probably one reason he was attracted to Taylor was that she was a spitfire, cut from a mold similar to Ash and Aunt Fiona, and his own mother, Julia. No wallflowers among the women he knew.

Taylor was more right for him than she knew.

Suddenly, Ash halted her big horse, wheeling around to glare at him. "What do you think you're doing?"

"What do you think *you're* doing?" Falcon asked. "Have you heard that there are mercs in the canyons who are known to kidnap Callahan women for sport?"

"I can take care of myself."

This was true. "Let me go with you. I'm feeling a need to ride and clear my head."

"And babysit me," Ash said disapprovingly.

"It's my sense of adventure. If I don't hang out with

you, I'll probably end up following in Tighe and Dante's footsteps."

"Traitors. Both of them."

"No." Falcon shook his head. "All of us have a destiny to follow."

"Whatever. *Destiny* is just a pansy word for shiftless. Lazy. Spineless. Maybe it was my destiny to get up this morning and eat chocolate chip cookies and drink beer for breakfast, but I didn't. I told Destiny to get the heck away from me."

"And ate rocks instead," Falcon said. "You have to forgive people who aren't as strong as you."

"Whatever," Ash said. "Tighe and Dante are strong. They just want to chase buckle bunnies. Their pride's a bit stung because they got smacked down by River and Ana. And right they were to turn my brothers down, since they're spineless weenies." She turned her horse and took off like the wind, riding across the flat land as if demons were after her.

Falcon checked his gun, made sure it was locked, and tucked it into his jeans. Then he followed his sister at a leisurely pace, his mind turning to Taylor again. Seemed as if he thought about her a thousand times a day. Maybe more.

It felt great.

TWENTY MINUTES LATER, Ash finally stopped her horse, slid off and tied it to a wizened tree where it could get a bit of shade and cool off in the late evening air. Falcon stopped next to his sister, knowing exactly what she was up to now.

"Looking at this land isn't going to do anything but make you hungrier for it," he said, dismounting.

"I like being hungry." Ash stared at the wide expanse of empty land. In the distance a small traditional adobe stood, marking the emptiness. "You're hungry, too, or you wouldn't have proposed to that town girl. You barely know her."

"I don't have to know Taylor. I like the way she looks." He watched as his sister pulled out small binocs and peered toward the farmhouse.

"It's going to be mine," Ash said. "You can propose to fifty girls, but this is going to be Sister Wind Ranch."

"Nice. But I have a different name in mind. Thanks."

She glared at him. "You don't have a name for it."

"I do."

"What is it?"

Okay, so he didn't have a name. He hadn't thought about it much. He just knew he hadn't wanted to get beat by his siblings in the race for the ranch. "It's on the tip of my tongue."

"And there it will stay. Fibber." Ash put away the binocs. "Come on. Let's walk to the farmhouse."

"Why?" He followed behind her. "This is private property."

"Yeah, it's private. Fiona owns it."

"Do we know that for sure?"

"She said the Callahan estate bought it."

He wasn't sure this was a good idea, but Ash had a determined tilt to her posture, so he went along for the adventure.

A man came out from the house and walked to meet them. "What brings you out here, folks?"

Ash glanced around. "I didn't know anybody still lived here."

"Of course I live here. This is my ranch." The white-haired farmer shrugged. "Been in my family for years."

"Oh." Ash looked concerned. "You didn't sell this property?"

"Thought about it. Had a couple offers. One from a little old woman who lives across the canyons, and a bigger one from an older gentleman who rode in here one day and told me whatever the old lady paid, he'd pay more."

"Was his name Wolf?" Falcon demanded.

"It was." The farmer nodded. "In the end, I decided I didn't want to leave my place. It's been in my family for years," he reminded them.

"I see," Ash said. "We're sorry to have bothered you."

"No bother at all." The rancher went off, his stooped body heading back toward the coolness of the adobe.

"Fiona told a whopper," Ash stated. "It's just like she did to our cousins. Got them married off, made sure there were lots of babies, then pow! So happily married they never battled for Rancho Diablo."

He laughed. "Let's not tell our brothers."

"Why not?" Ash looked at him as they walked back to their horses.

"It'll be fun to watch them work hard for something they're not going to get."

Ash mounted, waited for him. "I like the way you think. And now you can tell Taylor you don't need her anymore. You're a free man. There's no ranch to win. No ranch, no wedding."

He wasn't about to do anything of the sort. "So you're going to quit chasing Xav?"

"I don't chase him," Ash said. "And no, I'm not.

Pretty sure he needs the exercise. But Taylor might just let you catch her. And you wouldn't like that, Falcon. You know you aren't the committing sort."

They rode along in silence after that. Falcon tucked his hat down low on his brow, letting his horse follow Ash's. It was true. He wasn't the committing sort, and there was no prize. Fiona had set them up.

But Ash was wrong about one thing. He was certain he'd like Taylor letting him catch her. "I can keep a secret if you can."

"I'm not telling a soul. I'm going to watch Tighe and Dante run away from their *destiny,* and watch our other brothers get hitched and have families. Watching Fiona spin her web is fun, now that I'm onto her."

Falcon wasn't sure they weren't all caught in Fiona's web already. He was. But he didn't tell Ash, because Ash didn't believe in destiny.

He did. He wanted a date with destiny.

Chapter Three

Falcon waited on Taylor as she got off work, his game plan in hand. "Hi, beautiful."

Taylor stopped, turned to look at him. He leaned against his truck, giving her his best devil-may-care-and-be-damned smile. She studied him for a second, then walked over to him.

"What are you doing, Falcon? You look pleased with yourself, and I'm not sure that's a good thing."

He laughed. "Ride with me."

She raised a brow. "Why? And where?"

"Ride with me because I'm trying to bend Jillian's rules. Where—that's a surprise. A guy has to have some secrets. Then he's in touch with his feminine side, right?"

Taylor shook her head, clearly considering the wisdom of taking off with him. Falcon gave her plenty of time to talk herself out of it. He knew she wouldn't.

She might be taking Jillian's advice, but this little lady liked him. He could feel it.

"Didn't you agree not to date me?"

He smiled. "I said I wouldn't ask you to marry me. Dating's optional."

"I see." She considered that. "Where are you taking me?"

He reeled her in slowly. Taylor wasn't the average girl who'd be satisfied with a regular evening of food and awkward chat. "Ghost-busting."

She blinked. Hesitated.

He had her.

"Okay," she said. "But I can't be gone long. Maybe just an hour or two. I'm pretty sure we're not operating in the spirit of Jillian's challenge. You might be cheating."

He opened the truck door for her. "Might be. We'll see."

"It doesn't surprise me you'd bend the rules, to be honest, Falcon."

"Good guys finish last, they say." Sometimes that was true. Most times it wasn't. He was a good guy who intended to finish first, just as he always had. He drove for about twenty minutes, then turned down a deserted, dark road toward the canyons.

Taylor peered out the window. "So what are we really doing? Ghost-busting doesn't sound like your thing."

He smiled. "One thing you should know about me is that I never lie. We truly are looking for ghosts."

"There are no such things."

"Oh, Taylor. We're going to have to work on your appreciation for spirits."

She sighed. "I hope I don't regret doing this."

"What's life without a few regrets?" He stopped the truck several feet back from a narrow gorge he knew well. "Helps you appreciate life when you get it right."

"Whatever, cowboy. Let's go find this apparition of yours. It's dark enough for one to appear." She hopped out of the truck. "Not that I think you're doing anything but dragging me out here because you didn't want to go alone."

"Is there anything wrong with wanting a woman's touch on a ghost hunt? I heard paranormal phenomena are much more sensitive to a female presence. Or it could be that females just have better imaginations." He laughed at the eye-roll she performed for his benefit.

"All that time you sat at the bar watching me I never would have dreamed you have the soul of a romantic. Or something. So what game are you really up to?"

He took her arm. "Walking my romantic soul. Giving it a chance to breathe." Taking her in his arms, he kissed her on the lips, intending for it to be a quick one. But he found himself caught into lingering at the softness he encountered.

Kissing Taylor was so much more amazing than how he'd imagined it might feel that he didn't want to stop.

He pulled himself away with effort as Taylor stepped back.

"Is your soul done breathing?" she asked.

"For the moment." Falcon grinned, switched on a flashlight and pointed it on the ground. "Watch your step."

"I don't know how much longer I can stand the suspense," Taylor said. "It's well known in Diablo that you and your brothers and your sister, and all the Callahans, are pretty much one step from… Did you hear that?"

Falcon stopped beside her, swinging the flashlight toward the slight scuffling noise. "Probably just an owl."

"Owls don't land on the ground near people," Taylor said. "It's not really their desired activity."

"Okay, Nancy Drew. I was just trying to keep you from being scared."

"I'm not scared. I think you dragged me out here just to kiss me."

"Are you complaining?"

"Stating a fact."

"Fact noted." Beneath the banter, Falcon's radar was up. Taylor fell silent beside him, and he put a hand out to keep her near. He was packing a semi in his waistband so was prepared for anything, but the sound had been almost too deliberate to ignore.

It was like something was out there, following them. Years in the military had taught him caution, and he knew with sudden prescience that things weren't right.

"Where are we going, anyway?"

"I was going to show you the top of a cliff," Falcon said. "It's a full moon, and on a night like this you can see sky for miles from atop that cliff. You can see—"

His words broke off. "Falcon?" Taylor didn't move, her body suddenly tense. "Falcon?"

He'd been at her side a second ago, almost annoyingly overprotective. Now she couldn't feel him. It was as if he'd disappeared. There was no sound except the slight soughing of wind through the canyons. The flashlight was on the ground, pointing its beam toward black nothingness. Taylor picked it up and switched it off. She stayed completely still, listening.

There were three obvious scenarios here. Taylor considered her options. One, Falcon had brought her out here on a lark to give her a good scare, so she'd jump into his arms when he "rescued" her.

Fat chance. She wasn't falling for that.

Two, he'd stepped into a crevasse of some kind,

which had happened around here. Caves abounded in this area, and it was possible he'd simply disappeared into some hole—or they were nearer a canyon than he'd realized. But she'd have heard noise if he'd rolled down a gorge.

She discarded that notion. If he'd fallen into something, they were both in trouble because he had his truck keys. And she had no idea where she was, so walking back was out of the question. No one knew where they were, so this could turn into a tricky situation.

Next scenario: someone or something had grabbed him. Again, entirely unlikely, as Taylor felt certain she'd have heard signs of a struggle. A man as big as Falcon couldn't be easily dragged off in utter silence, and there would certainly be tracks.

Still, no matter what, she was in a less than desirable situation.

She could walk back to his truck and hope he hadn't locked it. There'd been a rifle on the rack, and likely he had bullets close by. She was a proficient shot, so she'd at least be safe.

Taylor swung the flashlight around her one last time, peering at the ground, making certain she didn't step into Falcon's possible Alice in Wonderland rabbit hole—and that's when she heard the definite sounds of all-out war.

She ran to the truck, grabbed the rifle, saw a box of ammo she gratefully snatched several bullets out of, and took off toward the ruckus. She tripped over something—probably an innocent rock—and forced herself to gather her wits enough to load ammo into the weapon. She crept forward, amazed when she spied Falcon fighting with an enormous man at the mouth of a cave, with two women acting as lookouts and one other male waiting to take a swing at Falcon.

Taylor took aim at the second man's foot, squeezed off a shot. He screamed and clutched his foot, and the two women pulled guns, crouching. When the big man's attention was caught by his friend's distress, he hesitated, and Falcon smashed him into a wall. The man slumped to the ground.

She liked these odds better. Taylor came out of hiding and walked into the cave, pointing the rifle at the two women. "Falcon's going to take your guns, ladies. I'm an excellent markswoman, so my best advice is for you to go sit back there, and take your bleeding friend with you."

"I thought you'd never come," Falcon said.

Taylor kept the rifle leveled at the two women, who headed off as she'd demanded. "You said we were ghost hunting. You didn't say you were looking for trouble in the flesh."

The big man on the ground began to revive, which seemed to encourage the man who'd removed his boot to stare at his bleeding foot. "You shot off my big toe," he told Taylor. "You'll be sorry."

She shrugged. "You've got one big toe left for balance. Keep talking, and I'll fix that."

"She's a tough one," Falcon told the four glaring at them. "I could have told you that. At any rate, we'll be going now. Would like to say it's been a pleasure, Uncle Wolf, but as always, it really hasn't."

He dragged Taylor from the cave.

"They're going to follow us," she said, gasping as they ran.

"It's okay. I've got some discouragement." He fired a

few rounds from a gun she hadn't realized he was carrying, so Taylor concentrated on getting to the truck.

"Give me your keys," Taylor said. "I'm driving."

"I like a take-charge woman." Falcon tossed her his keys and they jumped into the vehicle. Taylor shoved the key into the ignition, roared the engine to life and took off, praying no shots hit their tires or windows.

"This date didn't turn out the way I'd planned," Falcon said. "It's usually a little more exciting."

"I'm taking you to the hospital."

"Take me to the ranch," Falcon said. "My family will fix me right up."

She hit the main road, barreling toward Rancho Diablo. "Whatever you say."

"You know you want to go out with me again."

He was incorrigible. "Did I hear you call that man 'uncle'?"

"Yeah. Uncle Wolf is the black sheep of the family. Don't concern yourself with him. We don't have to invite him to the wedding."

She tried not to laugh out loud. Falcon was just so ridiculous. "I'm not marrying a man whose uncle tries to kill him."

"Why not? We make a great team. Has it occurred to you that maybe you're meant to be my guardian angel?"

Taylor pulled into the Callahan ranch, stopped the truck and looked at him. "You're bleeding a bit more than your aunt Fiona is used to seeing, I'm sure. Have a towel in the truck?"

"It's all right. Fiona's used to a few bumps and bruises. She doesn't panic."

Taylor could believe that. Between the six Callahans, and now their cousins, Fiona had probably seen her fair share of scuffed-up men. Taylor followed him into the house. "I guess that's good."

"Stick with me," he told her. "Life is an adventure."

"You don't say." She stared at Falcon, who was bruised and bleeding, but still the most handsome rascal she'd ever laid eyes on. "How could I ever refuse that offer?"

She wouldn't—and he knew it.

SO AS FIRST DATES WENT, it was a bit of a bust. Falcon readily admitted that. Still, Taylor had surprised him, even though she was known to be a capable, spirited woman.

He didn't think he'd made a great impression tonight. Of course he hadn't. And when Taylor told her mother and Jillian what had happened, he wasn't exactly going to come off as knight-in-shining-armor material.

"That's enough henpecking," he told his brother Galen, who was stitching the split skin above his right eye, where Wolf apparently had delivered a decent shot. "It's just a little knick."

Taylor leaned close. "Maybe more than a knick. Better sit still. Your brother's doing a pretty good job."

He smirked sourly, but minded the advice. He liked Taylor standing near him, and maybe if he sat still, she'd stay close.

"What did Uncle Wolf want?" Ash handed him a glass of whiskey he didn't really want, but when Taylor accepted a goblet of wine, he decided to be a good sport, too. Couldn't hurt to appear social; this was supposed to be a date, after all.

"He shared some dissatisfaction about the treatment he received from Sloan." He glanced over at his brother, who shrugged. Sloan was uncharacteristically mellow, despite the reference to Wolf kidnapping Kendall months ago.

Kendall smiled at Taylor. "Did Wolf have his dynamic duo with him? Two women who are generally unpleasant and have a thing for stealing great footwear?"

"Two women and another man. They didn't inquire about my boots, but honestly, plain brown Ropers might not be their thing."

Taylor leaned in to look at Galen's handiwork again, and Falcon caught a whiff of a sweet floral fragrance. He batted his brother away so only Taylor was close to him. "Let's go for a drive."

She looked at him, and he felt a tingling sensation way down in his soul.

"Again?" she asked. "Haven't you had enough adventure for one night?"

"I still want to count some stars with you." He didn't have much to offer her, but he was throwing a lasso around hope, anyway.

She smiled. "I need to get home to Mom."

He hadn't expected her to say yes, not after what had happened. "You're brave, you know."

"I know. Come on, drive me home."

His brothers shot him sympathetic glances, knowing he was batting zero. Falcon got up, resigned to the fact that she was never going out with him again, and trying to keep his disappointment off his face, which was sore enough at the moment without adding the persona of Droopy Dog to it.

Fiona sailed into the room, full of her customary good cheer. "Hello, everyone!" She enjoyed the chorus of hellos from her family, then glanced at Falcon.

"Rough night?" she asked.

"Perhaps a bit," he admitted.

"Well, we have those around here," his aunt said cheerfully. "Good to see you, Taylor. I talked to Jillian today."

Falcon glanced at Taylor, who was smiling at Fiona. He loved her smile. Just seeing Taylor looking happy made his face feel better.

"I understand you have a big date tomorrow night," Fiona said, "courtesy of Jillian."

Falcon's heart just about stopped. Taylor nodded.

"Not really a date," she said. "More like a cattle drive."

"With a state senator's son," Fiona said. "That's big game in these parts."

The whole room went silent. Falcon could feel his heart jump with a painful, stuttering beat. As if it was dying.

"It was great to see everybody again," Taylor said. "Falcon, can you drive?"

Of course he could—to the ends of the earth if she wanted. He grabbed his keys, trying not to look at the expressions of sympathy on his family's faces.

"Good night, everyone," Taylor said.

"Thanks for rescuing our brother," Tighe said.

"Yeah," his twin, Dante, said. "Falcon usually needs bodyguarding from the ladies. He wasn't expecting to get jumped by family."

This was all just great, Falcon thought with disgust. His own clan, helping his case not at all. He waved a hand to hush them, and he and Taylor left.

"You shouldn't have told them I shot your uncle's friend's toe off," Taylor told him as she got into his truck. "You exaggerated. I barely nicked him. Saying I got his whole toe makes me sound kind of mean."

"It makes you sound like a helluva woman," Falcon said.

"It was no big deal." She looked out the window, but Falcon knew it had been a big deal. Taylor had been honest when she'd said his gnarly family tree precluded serious consideration of marriage.

He really couldn't compete with the level of eligible bachelors Jillian was going to throw at his sharpshooting gal. He knew his wily aunt too well—she was in on it, too.

Everybody loved Taylor.

"I don't understand what they wanted with you."

Falcon wasn't certain, either. There was a possibility that Taylor could have been the target—like Kendall had been—but he doubted it. Wolf didn't usually make mistakes. "Wolf will do anything to get the ranch. If he could pick one of us off, or someone we care about, maybe we'll get scared and give up."

"You won't."

He shook his head. "It's not in our nature to give up. We're all stubborn that way." Pulling into her driveway, he switched off the engine. "I'll walk you to the door."

She opened her door and got out, turning to look at him only briefly. "That won't be necessary. I hope you heal fast, Falcon. Good night."

Taylor shut the door and took off into her house. She didn't even look back. Stunned, Falcon sat, amazed by how fast his evening had just ended.

But he got it. The whole evening had been awkward. No doubt weird, from Taylor's point of view. Of course it was weird. How many girls had to rescue their date?

He glanced at the rifle she'd left in the rack, just as it had been before, as if it had never been fired—but it had.

There was no changing what had happened. And tomorrow night Taylor had a date with Mr. Right.

Falcon pondered that for a moment, then realized what his next move had to be.

Chapter Four

"The thing is," Taylor told Jillian the next night, "I really think I could like Falcon except for all the obvious reasons not to. None of which my heart is paying attention to, of course, which is a very bad sign. This only happened to me once before, when I fell for a completely inappropriate man. Luckily, the insanity eventually passed."

Jillian put some glasses away behind the bar. "Callahans have been known to devastate the females of the population. I vote you gird your heart and go home and paint your toenails a pretty pink for your date." Jillian smiled at her. "You should know the phone's been ringing off the hook with men wanting to take you out."

"Why?" Taylor sank onto a bar stool. She really didn't want to go out with anyone besides Falcon. Then again, she wasn't sure she wanted to go out with him again, considering last evening. Jillian was right: dating a Callahan was fraught with complications. "Why do men want to take me out?"

"I'm not entirely sure, but I did hear a rumor that Fiona Callahan and her friends—conspirators, some call them—at the Books'n'Bingo Society decided this was the perfect opportunity to showcase Diablo's most eligible bachelorette. I think they rented a barn roof near the highway to advertise that we had a Diablo princess. Any eligible bachelor was invited to call a number for vetting. Fiona said they've had a hundred calls, and only found three worthy of the princess. I think she designated the process Pick-a-Prince. I'd call her tone pleased."

"The thing is," Taylor said, ignoring the thought of three unfortunate princes Fiona might foist on her, "when I saw Falcon fighting, so big and strong, I'm pretty sure my heart sat up and noticed. He was like John Wayne, but dark and somehow calling to all my forbidden desires. My heart definitely sat up, Jillian."

"Tell it to sit back down," she advised. "You don't need a fighter. You need a lover."

Taylor would bet Falcon could do both. Through the Diablo grapevine, she'd heard that he had taken those horses she'd been worried about to Rancho Diablo, and had a vet and farrier brought out to care for them. If that didn't warm a girl's heart, nothing would. She dusted off the counter and began wiping down booths. "He told me we were going ghost hunting, and then he disappeared, and my first thought was that he was rude for trying to scare me to death. You warned me he was a rascal." She sighed. "I think the evening might have scared up some of my own ghosts."

Jillian smiled. "Fear of commitment, fear of love, fear of falling for a big, handsome Callahan. You can't say I didn't warn you to try to avoid temptation. There's only one solution."

"I know. Paint my toenails pink for tonight."

"I'll even let you off early so you can get started.

The way to get your mind off one rascal is to get your mind on a different one."

Blind dates were the pits. Nothing good could come of it, especially when she had a yen for a dark-eyed rebel—a different kind of prince entirely.

"Now here's the deal," Fiona told her nephew, "I'm on your side. But you're going to have to be more forthcoming about some things. Right now it feels like we're at cross purposes."

Falcon put the saddle he was carrying onto one of the many split-rail fences that lined Rancho Diablo. "You're running the prince pick-a-thon for Taylor. How are you on my side?"

"Don't you worry about that." Fiona gazed up at her nephew. He stood a good foot above her, but Fiona always gave the impression that she was the more powerful force. Her white hair was pulled back in a no-nonsense knot from which a strand rarely came loose. She wore her customary rubber boots, which gave her traction, she said, for the ups and downs of a busy life. "I expect you to have plenty of gumption where Taylor is concerned. You won't disappoint me, I'm sure."

He leaned against a wood rail, recognizing his aunt had something on her mind. "Forthcoming about what?"

"What Wolf wants."

"I don't know."

She shook her head. "He didn't try to drag you off for a chat because he's the world's most caring uncle." Fiona touched Falcon's cheek lightly over the bruise. "I'm sorry this happened. But you're going to have to be straightforward with me."

"Says the aunt who's trying to fix up the woman

I like with a string of bachelors." He grimaced. "My guess is Wolf is trying to scare us. This is his second attack. Since he tried to take Kendall before, he either thinks he can get information from us, or he believes we'll get spooked. Spooked people make mistakes."

"Maybe." Fiona sat next to him on the rail. "I want you to take me to Wolf's hideout."

Falcon shook his head. "I can't do it. It's too dangerous."

"As your beloved aunt, I insist."

He sighed. "I know you do. It won't do any good. There's nothing there. My brothers and sister already paid the cave a visit."

"Find anything?"

"Not a thing. They were gone."

"Good." She hopped off the rail. "Then if nothing's there, you won't be worried about taking your aunt out for a small look-see."

"I'm not going to do it," Falcon said, "no matter how much I love you."

"I love you, too, but don't try to sweet-talk me, because this time it won't work. Let's go."

Falcon wondered if there was another family on earth whose aunt ruled the roost with such vigor. "I could be persuaded to compromise."

"You want me to end the search for Taylor's prince."

"Perhaps not be quite so enthusiastic about it."

She smiled, her eyes twinkling. "You're not afraid of a little competition, are you?"

He took a deep breath. "Look. I promised Jillian—well, I didn't really promise Jillian, she posed a challenge I thought was aggravating but respectable—that I wouldn't crowd Taylor. It's sort of a may-the-best-man-win thing. I have no doubt of my best-man status where Taylor is concerned. But it'd be nice if my aunt wasn't stacking the deck against me."

"I understand and can probably agree to your terms," Fiona said. "Partially, anyway. I have to take into consideration what's best for both of you, you know. Still, I've been known to parlay on occasion."

"You really want to see that cave, don't you?"

She nodded. "About as much as you want your girl."

Falcon wasn't really surprised. There was very little that didn't interest the redoubtable aunt. "Come on," he said. "Don't tell my brothers, and definitely not Ash, that I gave in to your gentle persuasion."

Fiona grinned. "I believe I have something of a reputation for being able to keep a secret."

Didn't he know it.

ASH MADE SURE HER POST was covered, then sneaked off to the canyons to hunt for her elusive crush. Xav Phillips was hiding from her and had been for months, though he wouldn't admit it. He'd taken over the outer perimeter of the ranch as his own personal post, though any of her brothers would be willing to take turns living in the canyons. Xav had exiled himself, and Ash had a strong suspicion it was because of her.

It didn't help that both his brothers, Shaman and Gage, and recently his sister, Kendall, had succumbed to the allure of marriage. Xav was determined to break the Phillips curse.

It wasn't just the Phillips curse. The Callahans had a real reason to wed. Fiona had thrown down a gauntlet, letting the seven Callahan siblings know that a great deal of land north of the canyons was up for grabs, a lottery to be won by the luckiest Callahan. You had to be married and have a family to quality for Fiona's raffle.

Everybody knew what Fiona had done to their six Callahan cousins—every last one of them hotfooting it to the altar for a stake at Rancho Diablo.

Ash wanted the land for Sister Wind Ranch, and Xav Phillips was her man.

But then she'd discovered that her aunt was cheating, trying to encourage them to get competitive and marry, though there was no "prize."

Still, Xav Phillips was her man. Even without the excuse of a holy grail, she wanted him more than ever.

She intended to do something about that.

Her brothers would be furious if they knew she was in the canyons without protection, especially after what had happened to Falcon. Ash didn't want to think about that.

She had to see Xav. It had been a solid month since she had. Never had she known a man who could go without creature comforts as long as he could, just to avoid falling in love.

She caught sight of Xav's horse, Omega, a big black gelding that complemented his owner. Xav wasn't in the saddle, which seemed a bit odd. He had to be close, so Ash cantered forward.

Xav's horse whickered at her when she rode alongside him. The horse eyed her almost thankfully. Glancing around, she looked for Xav. She didn't dare call out to him, and cell service would be dead here. "Where's your dad?" she asked the horse, but he seemed too tired to even shake his mane or move much. This wasn't like Xav's powerful horse at all.

Something was wrong.

The first thing she had to do was get this horse out of the searing heat and to water. Glancing around for an outcropping or any sort of shelter, Ash headed over to the nearest narrow carve-out she could find. Xav's horse followed, more like Eeyore than Trigger, and Ash's unease grew.

She saw Xav under the outcropping, lying faceup, eyes closed. He was so still she feared he might be dead. He shifted at the sound of horse hooves on the dirt-packed canyon floor, but didn't open his eyes.

"Xav?" Dismounting, Ash ran over to him. "What's wrong?"

He barely moved—but at least he lowered his arm and opened his eyes, turning toward her.

"Hey, Ashlyn."

"What happened?" She knelt beside him, glancing over his body. Everything looked fine—until she saw the blood leaking from his leg. "Did you fall?"

"Someone took a shot at me."

She had to get him help. "Can you walk?"

He didn't reply. She felt his forehead—fever, of course—swiftly thinking through her options. She could ride back for Galen and her brothers, but that would take time. Whoever shot Xav knew he'd gotten a good hit, and might be looking for him. There was no way she'd be able to lift him into the saddle, even if she could help him walk to his horse. By the amount of blood on his jeans, she guessed he'd been lying here awhile.

"I don't suppose you can walk."

He tried to lever himself up from the rock ledge, but although Ash pulled at his back, she couldn't support him, and he was too weak. "Okay, listen, Xav. I'm going to ride for—"

"Is something wrong?"

Ash gasped at the unexpected voice booming near her as Storm Cash walked up to the outcropping. The Callahans hadn't yet decided if he was friend or foe, though the vote was leaning toward the latter. Storm was certainly a handsome, rugged man, and he seemed nice enough to Ash—she hadn't picked up any hints otherwise—but someone had put a bullet in Xav. She looked at Storm, a bit of fear inside her.

"Xav fell off his horse," she said, not certain how much to share, and Storm glanced at Xav, concern etched on his chiseled face. No hint that he was the shooter coming to find his prey.

"Fell off?" He glanced at the blood crusted on Xav's jeans and pooled beneath him. "That's not like him." He knelt close to Ash, looking down at Xav. "If I help you to my horse, can you at least hang over the saddle?"

Xav gave a slight nod.

"I'll help you," Ash said, her heart racing. "We'll just put him on his horse. That way you won't have to follow us back—"

He looked at her. "His horse seems to be about done in. That's what I really came to check on."

She didn't mention that he was trespassing on Callahan land. This wasn't the time. Friend or foe, she needed Storm's assistance.

The mention of his horse being in trouble seemed to give Xav a vital boost of energy. He tried to raise himself to his elbows, and Storm helped him up from there. Though Xav was taller than Storm by a few inches and probably outweighed him by an athletic twenty pounds, Storm managed to get him to his horse. He helped Xav get his foot into the stirrup, then slump across the saddle.

"That's all we needed, buddy. We can take it from here." Storm turned to Ash. "Maybe we should get him to a hospital."

"I'm taking him to the ranch." Ash stood ready to defend this plan. "My family will decide what's best for him then."

"There's no telling how much blood he's lost. Maybe we take him to my ranch. I've got a—"

"Mr. Cash," Ash said, "Xav is going to our ranch. Thank you for the use of your horse, but if you have a problem with being on Callahan land, I'll take him myself and return your horse to you later."

"It's fine," Storm said. "Whatever you want."

He mounted his horse with Xav across the back and began walking. Ash watched Storm suspiciously, then mounted her own horse. To her relief, Xav's horse followed, even though it was a shadow of its normally vigorous self. Watching the terrain for any signs of danger, Ash stayed close to Xav, occasionally glancing at Storm.

How had he managed to coincidentally show up after Xav was wounded? She was so suspicious of him and so worried about Xav that her body felt flooded with adrenaline. Her brothers were going to kill her for being in the canyons. And they weren't going to be happy about her dragging Storm Cash to the house.

Her brothers didn't understand how she felt about Xav.

Storm waited for her to catch up to him. "I wasn't entirely honest about my reason for being back there."

A tickle of unease hit Ash. Worried, she glanced

toward Xav. He wasn't moving much. Was almost too still.

"Oh?" She didn't look at Storm.

"I'm afraid I followed you."

Her gaze jumped to him then. "Why?"

Storm shrugged. "Wanted to talk to you."

Maybe there was a logical reason behind the man's frequent presence at the ranch—beyond the overly friendly neighbor visits. "Something on your mind, Storm?"

"This may not be the best time to mention it, but you're pretty hard to get hold of, Miss Callahan." He glanced her way. "I was hoping you might accompany me to the Diablo Ball in December."

She blinked. *Awkward.* "I heard you'd proposed to Taylor Waters."

He nodded. "I did. She turned down my suit. So then I thought maybe my neighbor gal might want to accompany me. Sounds like it's going to be a real nice evening."

Xav looked as if he was trying to rise to a sitting position, though he wasn't going to make it. He muttered something, a string of incoherent words, and Ash looked at him with concern. "The less you move, the faster we can get you home, Xav. Your weight is too much on the horse," she told him. "Try to stay still."

After a few more twitches, he settled.

She looked back at the other man. "I don't know what to say, Storm. I wasn't planning to attend the charity ball." Of course she was—but she'd been planning to go solo, if she could talk Galen into letting her off post that night.

Xav made more noise, sounding like a pheasant startled from a forest. Of course, he was feverish, so that probably had a lot to do with his sudden flailing. No telling how long he'd been lying out there, bleeding.

He'd do anything to avoid her.

"Let me think about it, although I warn you my brothers will not be happy. But I did want to go, so thank you for the offer," she told Storm, and Xav fell silent at last.

"I THOUGHT I'D COME BY to talk to you," Taylor said to Falcon as she hopped out of her truck. "Unless you were about to leave?"

Fiona and Falcon did look as if they were about to take off somewhere. Taylor knew she should have called first. The thing about Rancho Diablo was that people felt comfortable dropping by whenever and often, and she'd decided to ambush her own nerves and just make herself go face Falcon. Spur of the moment. No phone call to make things more uncomfortable than they already were.

Now Taylor wondered if she'd been a bit too impulsive.

"We were about to leave," Falcon said, and his aunt nodded enthusiastically. "But you're welcome to ride with us."

Fiona turned and stared up at Falcon as if he'd lost his mind.

"You said you'd help me out," he told her.

"I didn't say we'd give away the family secrets," Fiona shot back.

"Maybe another time," Taylor said, and Falcon and Fiona both said, "No!"

"By all means, come with us," Fiona said. "We're just going to take a small joyride on the ranch."

"More ghost-busting?" Taylor asked brightly. "Falcon's big on ghosts." She got into the backseat of the military jeep.

Fiona sent her nephew a droll look. "Our whole family enjoys a good paranormal goose-pimpler."

The Callahans were legendary for their love of ghost stories and spiritual juju, according to her aunt Nadine. They even let a local woman give ghost-hunting tours on the ranch in the fall. Taylor smiled as they drove, listening to Fiona and Falcon banter. Fiona seemed very fond of her nephew, and just couldn't help ribbing him. Taylor's gaze focused on some horses making their slow way in the distance. Ash's platinum hair caught her eye, but she didn't recognize the man riding beside her. A third horse followed disconsolately behind the riders. "Who's that?" she asked, touching Falcon's shoulder. Through the black T-shirt she could feel muscles, strength—solidity so comforting.

"It's Ash," Fiona said. "And Storm."

"Never a good combination. Let's go throw a burr into whatever he's up to. Hope you don't mind, Taylor."

"Fine by me."

They pulled up alongside Ash and Storm, who came to a halt. Falcon cursed and jumped from the jeep. Fiona wasn't far behind her nephew, and Taylor followed, too, as they hurried to help Xav.

"What happened?" Falcon demanded.

"I found him pretty much unconscious," Ash said. "He'd dragged himself under a ledge. His horse was standing in the open, or I'd never have spotted him. Xav's been shot."

"What were you doing in the canyons?" Falcon demanded, examining Xav. "Help me get him into the jeep," he told Storm. "You can explain to me later why you always seem to be around when something's going wrong, Cash."

The two men lifted Xav from the saddle, gently carrying him to the jeep. "I'm going to run him to the hospital," Falcon said. "Fiona, I hate to abandon you—"

"I can take care of myself," she said. "So can Taylor. Hurry!"

Falcon left with Xav strapped in the passenger seat, quiet and pale. Taylor didn't know what to think about anything that had just happened. It was clear from Ash's face that she was shaken by Xav's condition.

"Come on, Fiona," Storm said. "I'll give you a lift."

"Thank you." Fiona sniffed, then allowed herself to be helped into the saddle behind Storm. "I think my nephew has a very salient point about you being around whenever there's trouble."

"Yes, ma'am," Storm said, and the two of them went off like bristling porcupines.

"Come on," Ash said to Taylor. "Let's get back to the ranch before my brothers come yelling at me."

Taylor took a hand up from Ash into the saddle. "Xav will be all right, Ash."

"I know."

Her voice was tight. Taylor could tell Ash was really worried. Xav hadn't looked all that good, sort of pale and obviously in pain.

"So what's going on with you and my brother?" Ash asked suddenly. "I thought the two of you were supposed to avoid one another until December."

"Falcon seems pretty good at bending the rules just enough to stay this side of honest."

Ash snorted. "Living outside the rules is pretty much a Callahan family trait. Serves us very well at times. The thing is, I don't know if my big brother's what you need in your life, Taylor."

Ash took off for the house, letting her horse run, soon galloping past Fiona and Storm. Taylor hung on, not sure what Ashlyn's words had meant—and not sure if they were friendly or not.

Chapter Five

Ash and Taylor slid off the horse as soon as they reached Rancho Diablo. "Galen!" Ash yelled at the top of her lungs. "Galen!"

Galen, Tighe and Dante came out of the barn closest to the house. "What?" Galen asked.

"Get to the hospital quick. Xav's been shot. Falcon took him there in the jeep."

Galen looked at Taylor and his sister. "Shot?"

"Yes. Would you hurry?" Ash's voice was desperate.

"I'm going." Galen glanced back just once. "You weren't in the canyons, were you?"

"We'll talk about that later," Ash snapped, and Galen disappeared.

Taylor thought it was a good time for her to disappear, too. Ash clearly wanted to tear out to the hospital, and she didn't want to be in the way. "When Fiona gets here, I'll catch a ride home with her. You go on," she told her.

"Oh, no, you don't," Ash said. "Don't go slinking off just yet. You and I are going to take a small drive. You know how to shoot, don't you?"

Taylor blinked. "Yes. Aren't you going to the hospital?"

"Not quite yet. We're going back to the canyons before anything's covered over. I want to find out who shot Xav. Wait until I get his horse some TLC, and then we'll head off."

Ash led the horses to the barn while Taylor stared after her. Maybe it wasn't the best idea to get caught up in Callahan issues.

Just then, Fiona and Storm rode up and Taylor helped Fiona slide down off the horse.

"Thanks for the ride," Fiona said.

"My pleasure," Storm replied.

"You're like some kind of funky genie, Storm," Ash said, appearing at Taylor's side. "You're always around when something's amiss. Just like Aunt Fiona said."

"Perhaps I was a bit harsh," Fiona said. "Storm has been very helpful."

Taylor thought Falcon's sister looked as if she wanted to debate the comment. But Ash clearly had other things on her mind.

"Are you going to the hospital, Fiona?" Ash asked.

"I'm going to get Burke, and then I'm off. Thanks again, Storm." Fiona went inside the house.

Storm tipped his hat to them and turned his horse.

"I'm watching you, Storm," Ash said. "Even if I accept your invitation, it doesn't mean we're going to suddenly be great friends."

"Yes, ma'am," he said mildly, and cantered away.

"I probably ought to get to Banger's," Taylor said.

"Do you have a shift?" Ash demanded. "Need to check on your mom?"

"No." Taylor didn't have anything pressing. All she'd planned to do was ghost-bust with Falcon, which in retrospect seemed like a bad idea. The only ghosts around here were the ones in Falcon's head. "I have a date—"

"Good," Ash said, interrupting her. "You can cover me. Come on," she said, climbing into the jeep.

"If I'm going to cover you," Taylor said, "you can explain what you meant about your brother not being what I need in my life."

Ash started the ignition. "There's a small gun in that box," she said, pointing to the jeep floor. "It's basically a pop gun, it'll give you a chance to create a diversion. As for my brother, all I'm saying is that Falcon's very bright. Very courageous. Thinks too much. Really, it's his only fault." She sounded very cheerful about Falcon's list of defects. Her platinum hair blew in the breeze, her curls dancing. "A little out there. I know he proposed to you. That's what I mean. Very odd, right? While you," she said, glancing over at Taylor, "strike me as being a bit more pragmatic. Conventional."

"Are you saying I'm too boring for Falcon?"

Ash drove a bit faster, flying over ruts in the rough ground. "Yes."

"So you're trying to talk me out of accepting his proposal."

"No. I'm just saying opposites attract, but likes stay together."

"Just so long as it's not personal or anything. Or your opinion isn't based on that ranch all of you want so badly. I mean, you wouldn't be trying to knock your brother out of the competition, would you?"

"Maybe *knock* is a harsh word. Beat my brothers competitively, of course. But if you're crazy about Falcon, then far be it from me to dissuade you from accepting him." She seemed pretty blithe. "They're so protective of me that I feel it's my duty to be protective of them in return."

Taylor grinned. "Sure you do."

"We'd be sisters, you know." Ash halted the jeep near the bunkhouse that had recently been completed near the canyons. "I hope you're as good a shot as I've heard. Wolf's buddy is still complaining that you shot his toe off. We hear about these things at Rancho Diablo."

"It wasn't his toe." Taylor put the binocs to her eyes and scanned the seemingly endless landscape. "It was barely the tip of his boot. If I'd wanted his toe, I'd have hit it."

"You know," Ash said thoughtfully, "Falcon was a decent sniper in the military."

"Decent?" Taylor put the binocs down and looked at her.

"Decent as in has his share of decorations." Ash looked proud of her brother despite her modesty. "He probably likes a woman who could handle a weapon."

"I think you've already put me off your brother." Taylor got down from the jeep. "Let's go see what we can scare up."

Ash followed. "Let's go to the overhang where I found Xav."

Taylor scanned the ground, seeing dried blood, footprints and a spent shell casing. "There's that bit of information you wanted."

Ash looked down. "That makes no sense. Can I pick it up with my hands, or should I use something in case of fingerprints?"

"I'd say if the bullet matches the casing, then that's information enough for the police to trace the gun owner, if the bullets were bought locally."

"But if it's not a registered rifle," Ash said, "better be safe than sorry." She grabbed the cap she kept in the car to keep the sun off her face, and scooped up the evidence.

Taylor didn't want to jump to conclusions, but there was certainly something fishy about all this. "Let's get to the hospital. Give me the cap and I'll hang on to it while you drive. We don't want anything to happen to the—"

They both jumped when Wolf walked up to them. "Hello, ladies."

Taylor slapped the cap on her head, feeling the bullet casing rest against her scalp.

"You're trespassing, Uncle," Ash said. "Again, damn it. Seems to be a recurring problem you have. Maybe you need one of those shock collars that people use on their dogs when they won't stay in the yard. Only this collar would be to keep you off Callahan land."

He smiled, but it wasn't genuine. "Well, this is the lady who's so handy with a gun. My buddy Rhine has part of his toe missing thanks to you."

Taylor kept silent.

"What do you want, Uncle?" Ash demanded.

"I lost something around here. Wonder if you've seen it?" He glanced around the area, his gaze passing over the dried blood as if it was of no importance. Which told Taylor everything she needed to know.

"I'm late for my evening of cattle driving," she told Ash. "I'm sorry I can't stay longer. You and your uncle will have to excuse me."

"Hang on, doll face. I'm not done talking to you."

"You are," Falcon said, coming up behind his uncle. "Doll face is late for her date, like she said."

Taylor thought Falcon was probably everything Ash claimed: stealthy, dangerous, ominous. Fully a match for any situation.

Wolf smiled at her. "Looks like we'll have to talk another time, Miss Waters, Diablo's own resident princess."

So he'd checked up on her, knew who she was. A slight tingle of fear ran over her. "Whatever."

"Say hello to your aunt and your mother for me," Wolf said as she departed, Ash not far behind.

"That's enough," Falcon said. "You're a broken record, Uncle. Let's send you on your way home."

Falcon watched his uncle mount his horse and gallop off. Then he walked back toward the women, and the first thing Taylor thought was how handsome he was, how strong and sexy.

Her second thought was that judging by the look in his navy eyes, he was not happy. Annoyed, even.

With *her*.

"How's Xav?" Ash asked, her voice eager.

"I'll tell you everything when we get back to the ranch," Falcon said, "and out of the canyons. Again."

"Oh." His sister sounded a bit despondent. Taylor guessed it wasn't the time to bring up the spent shell. Whatever was bugging Falcon didn't seem as if it might be assuaged by talking about *evidence*.

"You ride my horse," Falcon told his sister. "I'll drive the jeep. I have something I want to discuss with Taylor. In private."

"Okay. I want to go check on Xav. I guess I'll take my cap back from you, if you don't need it, Taylor." Ash shot her a sympathetic glance that clearly said *You're in hot water.* "I've got some other lighter caps in my room you can borrow if you need one that isn't heavy as *lead.*"

Clearly, Ashlyn was trying to help her out of the tight spot she was apparently in with her brother. Taylor slipped the cap off, capturing the shell, and handed it to Ash, who gave her a wry look.

"Have fun," Ash said.

"Thanks. Troublemaker."

Ash laughed, and Taylor went to face Falcon.

"HERE'S THE THING," Falcon said, leading Taylor to a private place in the main house where they could talk, which for the moment happened to be the basement. Taylor's eyes were huge, taking in Fiona's stocks of canned vegetables and fruits, and the myriad boxes of her much loved, carefully labeled seasonal ornaments. "I don't want you letting my sister drag you into stuff."

"Falcon, I know you're worried, but it was no big deal. It wasn't Ash's fault."

"Taking you to the canyons wasn't her fault?"

"Okay, that was, but nothing else." Taylor put on an innocent face he suspected was meant to diffuse his focus. It nearly worked, too.

"What nothing else?"

"Whatever you're mad about."

"I'm not mad, Taylor. I'm concerned. I feel responsible for you."

She blinked. "Don't."

"If something happened to you, your mother and Jillian would question my ability to protect you."

"That's what this is all about. Your sense of macho is disturbed."

"My sense of macho is *never* disturbed." He wondered how he could explain to this darling woman that he was required by man law to protect her. "There's a lot going on at this ranch you don't understand."

"I bet." She looked at the long, narrow strip of packed dirt near the wall. The spot always reminded Falcon of a coffin. The dirt floor had apparently always bugged Jonas Callahan, but it was there due to foundational issues or something. Jonas had had the new two-story bunkhouse near the canyons built with a perfectly-floored basement.

No room for secrets.

"You're missing part of your floor," Taylor said. "It's kind of strange, isn't it? Looks like a coffin might be buried there."

Falcon felt as if a goose had walked over his grave. "Apparently Uncle Jeremiah built this place with a few holes."

"Seven chimneys, and he left holes in the basement floor?" She looked at Falcon. "You Callahans don't do a thing to diminish the legend, do you?"

"We're talking about you, not me, beautiful. No more canyons. No more letting Ash lure you into her adventures. I'm tame compared to my sister."

"I wouldn't have suspected you of being a bore, Falcon." Taylor went over to the gash in the floor and moved some dirt aside with her boot. He watched her carefully, pretty sure she was trying to tweak him, and succeeding mightily. Telling her to quit messing around would get her suspicions up, and she seemed to have a strong dose of Miss Marple in her.

"Maybe this is a grave," Taylor said, glancing at him with a teasing smile. "There's wood underneath the dirt. Are you hiding vampires in your basement, Falcon? Is that why Callahans are known to be fond of ghost hunts and stories?"

Well, she was getting close on a lot of levels. She was just too cute and too witty for her own good—a ball of mischievous intent.

There was only one way to stop her sudden fixation with the floor she was rapidly uncovering. He hated to do it—surely it was bending the rules—but a man had to do what a man had to do, and besides, if anybody was born to be a rule buster, surely it was him.

He pulled the busy Miss-Marple-in-the-making into his arms, kissing her until she gasped with surprise and pulled back.

"Falcon!" She stared at him. "What are you doing?"

"Breaking the rules?" He went back to kissing her, and this time she didn't pull away.

In fact, she kissed him back, pretty enthusiastically, he thought.

His blood screamed with desire. She felt so good in his arms, everything he'd ever dreamed of and more. All those long months of staring at her in the bar, fantasizing, wishing, knowing it was all so impossible…

Impossible was in his arms, suddenly hot and surely possible.

Forbidden fruit was the best—no doubt about that.

He ran his palms over Taylor's lush backside—my God, it was the stuff of dreams—and she moaned, pressing up against him with those generous breasts he'd tried many a time to stop surreptitiously checking out. She was just so much woman, an hourglass-shape of delight, and thankfully, she'd forgotten all about the basement floor and seemed focused on him.

Her hands were just as busy as his. It was as if she

couldn't get enough of him, which made Falcon hotter than the fire in the stone circle in the canyons. He was going to take her to that circle one day, show her the setting of stones, one for each Chacon Callahan sibling. And he was going to make love to her right there, in the home of his spirit.

She reached for his belt buckle, shocking him when she undid it with deft, eager fingers—and it hit him that all his lucky stars were falling out of the sky on him, blessing him with something he'd never, ever had the courage to imagine.

He was going to make love to the best girl in Diablo—right here, right now—right next to Rancho Diablo's buried treasure.

It wasn't breaking the rules if no one ever found out.

She whispered, "Falcon…" against his neck, and he went spinning over the edge, into the hot heaven that was Taylor.

Chapter Six

"So, did Falcon yell at you? Much?"

Ash's blue eyes were huge in her sun-warmed face, worried as she was about her big brother's overprotective fit yesterday. Taylor kept walking down the sidewalk on the main drag in Diablo, carrying her sack of groceries, everything right in her world. "He yelled, sort of. Not as much as you'd imagine. In fact, Falcon's really more of a lover than a fighter."

Ash tagged along beside her. "You don't know Falcon. He's totally a fighter. In fact, of all of us, he's a little bit crazy, if you know what I mean. I was worried about you."

"Why? He's a kitten."

Ash stopped in her tracks for a moment, then caught up again. "Never let Falcon hear you say that. He sees himself more as a stealthy tiger. In fact, his spirit aura is—"

"Ash, quit worrying." Taylor went into Banger's and set the groceries on the counter for Jillian. "How is Xav?"

"He's fine. They did a surgery to take out the bullet. He wouldn't take any pain meds. Said he had to live up to the Callahans, or something stupid like that. One of us hypnotized him so he wouldn't feel pain, but I'm not saying who, so don't ask. He's pretty happy now, except he wants out of the hospital yesterday." Ash's face glowed as she bragged on Xav. "I'm crazy about him."

"I know. He knows." Taylor smiled.

"You think that's a bad thing?" Ash looked anxious.

"Not in his case. He's running from himself, not you, is my guess."

Ash raised a brow. "You sound like a Callahan. Philosophical."

"I don't quite ladle around all the balone—I mean, thank you." She smiled at Ashlyn. "I'll take that as high praise. What did you do with the casing?"

"Oh. I gave that to Sheriff Cartwright. Then I had to tell my brothers I'd found it." She sighed. "Of course, you found it, but I covered for you. Falcon was annoyed enough."

"Thanks."

"Whatever. Don't act like you're grateful, because I know you weren't really worried about Falcon's temper."

Taylor smiled. "Actually he seems like a reasonable individual."

Ash shook her head. "You'll have to learn the hard way. I've got to go. Thanks for going with me yesterday."

"It was fun."

"Not really," Ash said. "I'm sorry I got you yelled at."

"I'm just glad everything turned out for the best."

Ash sniffed. "You know, Taylor, Jillian is right."

It was a little too late if Ashlyn was going to warn her off Falcon again. "What have you got against your brother?"

"Nothing," she said hastily. "He's a great guy. It's

just you've been raised gently, kind of the town princess, you know? And Falcon's more the badass from nowhere. I don't see how it works."

"You're a rebel, and you're running after Xav, who's—"

"Become a very good rebel." Ash beamed. "They say that there was a time when all he lifted were corporate agreements, and he never saw more than ten minutes of daylight at a time. I'm really proud of him."

"Okay. So you're a match. Don't worry about me and Falcon. As you say, he's got a heart of stone, and I've got a date tonight. No worries."

"Really?" Ash's nose wrinkled.

"Yes," Taylor said, sighing. "Some suit from some big corporation Fiona knows is flying in tonight."

"Suits are dangerous," Ash said. "Suits can *change*."

Well, Xav had, but that wasn't true of all suits. "You said I should be looking for something other than your brother. Don't try to turn me away from my destiny."

"Destiny?" Ash backed away. "Oh, no. Messing with it is unwise. It's bad juju. People don't understand that. They always want to out-think their intended future. It leads to all kinds of heartache. Trust me, I know whereof I speak. I tell people I don't believe in destiny, but one should never tempt it. I try not to tempt it by ignoring it."

Taylor smiled. "Bye, Ash."

Ashlyn shot out the door, and Taylor went home to dress, not at all happy about her big date.

Taylor had a problem. She wasn't interested in meeting Fiona's Prince Charming in a suit. Because she was certain she'd already met her destiny—in the arms of a big, overbearing cowboy who just happened to melt her with sweet kisses and his oh-so-obvious need to be tamed.

"WHAT DO YOU MEAN, she has another date?" Falcon glowered at his sister. "Taylor can't have a date, she and I just made—" He stopped himself from saying *made mind-blowing love in the basement,* and lowered a frown on his sister instead.

Ash didn't seem impressed.

"I heard it from her own lips. She's going out tonight with a corporate suit Fiona dug up for her. You're going to have to talk to the redoubtable aunt to find out more. All I know is that the suit is supposedly taking Taylor to a restaurant in Tempest, which is only a few minutes away, really, if you're driving a very fast truck. And as I recall, we have oodles of family in Tempest, at Dark Diablo ranch, don't we?"

"Fiona's supposed to be on my side." Falcon slumped onto a kitchen bar stool in the main house.

"Good luck with that." Ash swiped a cookie off the platter in the center of the counter and munched happily. "No one's ever certain what side our aunt is on. She's sort of a wild card, if you think about it. You can draw her, but once you've got her in your hand, she could go either way. Very dicey, as aunts go."

"I just don't see how Taylor can have a date." Falcon shook his head. The woman had literally romanced his socks off yesterday. She'd been a fireball in his arms, wrapping her legs around him, fiercely whispering his name with little whimpers of delight.... He broke off the memories he'd been savoring all day.

"Reality is harsh at times," Ash said brightly. "Anyway, you cooked your own goose, brother, gravy and all. You're the one who graciously agreed that you wouldn't press your suit until December, while Jillian and Fiona found any number of Prince Charmings to win her away. Talk about giving away the prize. Over-confident much, brother?"

"I was trying to be a gentleman," Falcon growled. "I was trying to live within the rules. I didn't count on my aunt sandbagging me."

"Well," Ash said, smiling with obvious glee, "you both agreed to the rules, so put your tiny whiney fiddle away. I'm off to see my adorable cowboy. They think they're going to send Xav home tomorrow, so I only have one more day to captivate him while he's a…captive audience."

She was far too pleased with herself. Falcon sighed. "Give me some advice I can use here. I know very little about the female species. I really thought Taylor dug me just a bit."

"Why?" Ash cocked her head. "Because you yelled at her for going into the canyons with me? Because you treat her like she's on a pedestal, so everyone else will, too, thus recognizing her untouchableness?" Ash gave him a sisterly pop on the arm. "You'll figure it out, bro. Slowly, but you will. I've given you all the help I can, but now it's visiting hours. Bye!" She went off, humming.

Sometimes Ash was the world's most annoying little sister. Falcon was positive very few brothers had a sister who deviled them to the extent that she did. Sometimes he was certain she was setting him up for a fall. Other times she was an angel, reaching out a hand to help him up.

The females in his life were driving him mad.

Then it hit him hard exactly what Ash had given him.

A challenge.

"WHY ARE WE HERE instead of our lazy brother?" Dante asked Tighe, as they sat in the dark booth in the comfortably dark restaurant in Tempest, New Mexico. He was speaking only half in jest about Falcon, who'd sent them on this spy mission. "Keeping an eye on Taylor is *his* job. So once again, why are we—"

"Because," Tighe said, eagerly attacking the bowl of bread the curvy waitress put before them, "he's our brother. And Falcon's been rather unmanned by his emotions for Taylor, if you hadn't noticed, which would be impossible not to notice, because just about everybody in Diablo is talking about our much-decorated brother, who could handle anything the military threw at him, completely cratering under the sweet, burning torch he's carrying for Taylor."

"You almost have the loquacious style and wit of a philosopher of yore," Dante said, annoyed, "except you didn't really answer my question. Why us?"

"Simple, Watson. We're spies." Tighe grinned. "As your twin, I don't hesitate to say that I'm the better spy, naturally. I was first from the womb, I was first in the sack races in first grade, I also beat you at—"

Dante held up a hand. "Sweetheart, can you get me another Shiner? And if you want to toss some aspirin on the side, that'd be real helpful, darling. My brothers are trying to drive a stake through my skull."

The waitress gave him a smile that lit up the room. Dante smiled back, but not with as much wolfish warmth as he might have if he didn't have his own little crush going. He was in as good a position as Falcon, un-requited love and all that, but not near to beer-weeping, which sometimes he thought Falcon was getting close to, if he didn't stop being such a drama dude.

Dante glanced over at Taylor and her date. "I get why Falcon digs her so much. Taylor's smarter than he is. She's better looking than him, too. And she's unattainable."

"The shiny object," Tighe said cheerfully, almost amused by their brother's emotional pain. "The Holy Grail that calls to a man, whispering of soft, perfumed nights and heaven heretofore undiscovered."

"Great gravy," Dante muttered. "Why was I saddled in the zygote with you?"

"I've always wondered about that vanishing-twin thing. I think, why couldn't my twin have disappeared into thin air?" Tighe popped the last bite of his bread into his mouth with satisfaction. "Which is probably why Mom said I kicked you all the time. I was trying to kick you out of the womb. That's the reason I was born first—I was trying to escape your ham-headedness. Now, as for Taylor, all you need to know about our dating darling over there is that our brother is head over heels in love with her. We can help him out…or not."

Dante lowered his brows. "What do you mean?" He gobbled the ibuprofen and the beer the precious little waitress set on the table. "We're here. We're helping."

"Does us no good whatsoever if Falcon should catch said shiny object," Tighe pointed out, jerking his head toward Taylor.

Dante felt his jaw become slightly unhinged. "You're not suggesting that we sabotage our brother?"

Tighe shrugged. "You want that land or not?"

"I don't know." Dante sighed with pleasure as a huge steak was set in front of him. There were steaming mashed potatoes with a generous dollop of butter, a brightly colored vegetable mix, and if Tighe would quit talking, he'd be the happiest man on the planet. "I wasn't just threatening about hitting the rodeo circuit with you."

"Me, either. That doesn't mean we're giving up the race for the land. It just means we don't tie ourselves to the future of Rancho Diablo."

Dante's fork hung over his steak. "I'm going to regret this, but you're speaking a bit of family treason, bro."

"Rancho Diablo is not our home," Tighe pointed out. "What's she doing right now?"

Dante glanced back over at Taylor. "Uh, the city dude is kissing her fingers, like he's French or something. Taylor isn't smiling. She looks bored."

"Well, finger kissing is boring." Tighe dug into the huge pile of lasagna on his plate. "Mmm, at least we're getting great eats on our brother's nickel."

"You're not suggesting that we turn our backs on our cousins? Our family?"

"Sure." Tighe shrugged. "We've been guarding Aunt Fiona and Rancho Diablo for over a year. We've done our family duty. If we're going to take a shot at our dream, we need to get to it. We're not getting any younger, and bulls are not easy on an old man's body. And I don't particularly want to get shot up like Xav Phillips over a battle that isn't ours."

Dante took another quick peek back at Taylor. She'd pulled her hand away from her suitor, who was obviously trying to figure out how to get her into bed, and thought if he started slowly with fingers, he might work up to more. As if that ever worked. Dante snorted to himself. *Loser. With moves like that, it would take him six months to get a girl in the sack.*

Then again, Dante wasn't having much luck with the woman he had his eyes on. When Kendall Phillips had returned to set her cap for Sloan, she'd brought a deluxe model of female hotness with her—two bodyguards to protect Kendall's darling twin newborns. All so Kendall could be close to Sloan, who was bent and determined that the way to win his woman was to send her and his children to another state. Kendall had outsmarted Sloan with the sexy, tough bodyguards—and Dante and Tighe had promptly felt their hearts, their collective practical reasoning and their vaunted bachelorhood status itch to go the way of the dodo. Gone.

But the bodyguards, Ana and River, hadn't given them the time of day. *I'm not doing any better than City over there. I didn't even get to kiss Ana's fingers—although to be fair, I would have started with her toes and worked my way up.*

He sighed, bit into his steak. "I almost get your premise. You're working on two. You're saying that this isn't our fight, so we're not obligated. And you're also positing that we don't do our job tonight, which is keeping an eye on our brother's crush." Dante poked his fork in the air. "I'm not entirely shocked by your disloyalty and your competitiveness, because sometimes your competitive side overwhelms your good sense, but you're forgetting a few things."

"Tell me where I'm wrong," Tighe said, inhaling his lasagna. "Tell me you haven't chafed a bit under our grandfather's grip on our life."

Dante glared. "I do not chafe. I serve."

"So? What's it getting you?"

"It's not supposed to get any of us anything. Let me tell you what the frogs in this theoretical pond of yours are. One, we don't turn our back on family. Ever. It pains me that I shared a zygote with you if you're being this disloyal. Just because you want to leave and haven't quite talked me into it doesn't mean you're getting close." He glared at his brother. "Second, even if I wanted to tell Running Bear that I was handing in my family membership—because that's what we'd be doing—I could never turn my back on Fiona and Burke. Nor my cousins, either, but particularly the older folk." He got sad just thinking about it. Fiona needed them. She thought she could handle everything herself, but Fiona was no spring chicken.

She was independent, though. If she had half an idea of how Tighe felt, she'd send him away to chase his dreams with a basket of cookies and a cheery smile.

"As for throwing a wrench in our brother's love life," Dante said with a shrug, "there's no need. There are plenty of wrenches to keep him busy without us getting involved, practically an entire toolbox full. No need to play dirty." He drank some beer and thought his headache was starting to recede just a bit, thankfully. If he could get Tighe to stop spinning webs of his own glory, maybe he could concentrate on what a really good meal this was, how it had been a pleasant night for a drive, and how he was ever going to talk Ana into letting him kiss her, anywhere at all on her luscious body.

Hell, he'd even settle for her fingertips.

TAYLOR WAS SO JUMPY she could hardly enjoy the evening, which she'd known wasn't going to be a lot of fun.

She wasn't the adventurous kind of girl who enjoyed blind dates. But Tighe and Dante sitting over in the corner booth weren't helping the situation at all. The waitress had pointed them out, mentioning the good-looking cowboys from Rancho Diablo, and how she'd love to put just one of them in a doggie bag and take him home.

Taylor hadn't been amused in the slightest, although Benton had laughed appreciatively. Was it coincidence that Tighe and Dante were here? Surely it was. Falcon wouldn't send his brothers to spy on her.

Besides, Falcon hadn't known where her date was taking her tonight.

Ash had known.

It didn't matter. Not comfortable with the whole blind date thing, Taylor was now just short of patience with her beau. Benton H. Withers III wasn't a bad-looking man at all, if one liked big, handsome, sandy-haired guys. But she'd been romanced by a dark-haired rogue, and it made poor Benton pale by comparison.

Darn Falcon, anyway. Benton was a perfectly suitable dinner companion.

She was bored stiff.

"Dessert?" Benton asked. "It's a very tempting offering they have here."

He looked eager to try something on the dessert menu. Taylor smiled, trying to seem enthusiastic. "Go ahead. I'm full, but it would be fun to see what they have." She tried not to glance over at Tighe and Dante again. The problem with Callahans was that they were bigger than life, so they tended to suck up all the attention wherever they were.

"Share a slice of mocha chip ice cream pie with me," Benton said.

The man had flown from New York for this dinner, thanks to Fiona and her merry band of meddlers. "That sounds lovely," Taylor said, even though she was working on a headache the size of Mount Olympus.

"You should come to New York for our next date," Benton said, and Taylor nearly choked on the tea she'd been sipping. She looked at him with alarm.

There was never going to be another date with Benton of the pristine portfolio and dapper, streamlined looks.

And that's when Taylor decided that if she had to live through three months of blind dating and empty dinners with perfectly nice men whom she could never kiss good-night without feeling completely guilty about Falcon, she was going to have to make a serious change in her life.

Darn Falcon and his sexy-hot, irresistible lovemaking, anyway.

Chapter Seven

"Dude, that was a delicious dinner," Dante said, throwing himself onto a leather couch in the upstairs library, and looking, Falcon thought, like a man who'd thoroughly enjoyed setting fire to the two hundred bucks he'd given his brothers for dinner—with a little extra for bribery. Just to make certain to keep their focus strictly on Taylor, and not on any sweetly shaped bit of temptation that happened to bounce across their vision, which happened with Tighe and Dante. One had to factor in their lack of concentration and plan accordingly.

"Well?" Falcon asked in a growl. His brothers and sister laughed at him, making no attempt to conceal their mirth.

"When I told you where the big date was going to take place, I didn't expect you to send emissaries," Ash said. "You weenie."

"I'd have looked like a real weenie if I'd shown up in Tempest," Falcon pointed out. "A real schmuck weenie with a jealous streak."

"Oh, that wouldn't describe you at all," Ash said, her expression innocent.

"That's right," he said, "so I sent Howdy and Doody."

"That's not nice," Tighe said. "We kept an eye on Taylor, painful as it was."

"Painful?" Nothing hurt so much as his heart at the moment. Falcon was about to die of jealousy, though he'd never admit that to his gloating sibs.

"Well, it was all the romancey-schmancey stuff," Dante said. "The finger-licking and the cooing."

"Cooing?" Falcon sat up straight, knives spearing his heart. His family had no sympathy, practically rolling with laughter. He didn't care.

"You know." Tighe waved a hand grandiosely. "The sweet nothings being whispered in the delicate ear. That sort of cooing."

"Did he have delicate ears?" Falcon demanded.

Dante glared. "We didn't look at date number two's ears. Our assignment was to keep an eye on Taylor, which we did, without deviation. Dinner was fabulous, by the way. Gained ten pounds, I'm sure of it. And when we saw them splitting a dessert, we went for all the trimmings ourselves. I would drive to Tempest every day of the week just to eat that mocha chip—"

"They *shared* a dessert?" Falcon jumped off the sofa, paced to the windows. That wasn't supposed to happen. He'd made love to Taylor, every inch of her, every delicious curve and delightfully sensitive spot. His heart was *breaking*.

"This isn't a good idea," Galen said, his tone worried. "Falcon, you can't send spies to watch Taylor."

Falcon blinked. "I can't?"

"No," Sloan said, "you have to catch her without hijinks."

"Like you did with Kendall?" Falcon shot back.

"What he means," Jace said, "is that it's not cricket."

"I don't care about crickets. Ash gave me a challenge, I tended to it in the best way I knew how. At great expense, too." But even Falcon knew he shouldn't have done it. He sighed to himself, feeling fairly downcast. "I shouldn't have let you tweak me," he told his sister.

"I thought you'd go in person and show the poor guy up," Ash said. "I didn't think you'd turn into a shadow of your former self and cave to the competition."

"Crap," Falcon said, drooping a bit. "I gave Jillian my word I'd leave off proposing to Taylor until the Christmas season. She could date other people and if she found something better—which is Jillian's goal—I'd accept that."

"Dummy," Ash said gently, "you weren't supposed to let her get swept away by the something better. Instead, you sent Howdy and Doody. How does that make you look like Prince Charming?"

"I don't know." Falcon got up, honestly confused. "I quit. I give up." He was too devastated to think straight anymore.

His family stared at him, their faces shocked.

"What did you say?" Galen asked.

"What?" Falcon said. "What do you mean, what did I say?"

"That horrible thing you said," Jace said. "Something like *I quit. I give up.*" He shuddered.

Falcon was done talking about the whole matter. "Are we having a family meeting or not? Is anybody going to give an update on Xav? Or are we just going to sit around in a hen session?"

They continued to look at him in confusion. Falcon shook his head, and departed with his seriously unhappy heart.

"THAT DIDN'T GO WELL," Galen said. "Think you laid it on a bit thick, Howdy?"

"What?" Dante asked, his expression too innocent to be genuine.

"Thick? Every word was true." Tighe clearly intended to back his twin up to the max.

"Did you really think telling Falcon where Taylor's date was would be helpful?" Galen demanded of Ash.

"How did I know he'd muff up the mission?" She frowned at Galen. "Falcon should have gone himself."

"Why?" Galen shook his head. "Look, I can't bear him moping around looking like someone ripped his favorite blankie. He's not going to be any good here if his heart is broken, and I don't know about any of you, but I could hear it splitting clear across the room."

Dante and Tighe looked slightly ashamed of themselves. Ash, as usual, did not. Galen sighed. Sometimes it was like herding cats to get his siblings to think logistically and without the liberal dose of turkey juice that seemed to clog all their thought processes.

They were, in a word, impetuous. Hotheaded.

And he hated to admit it, but...wild. Like coyotes in the wilderness.

He didn't know how he was going to keep this ragtag bunch of misfits focused on the mission.

"By the way, Dante and I are turning in our notice," Tighe said. "We're hitting the rodeo circuit. This is our official notice."

Galen's ears rang and he felt his forehead pinch together in a frown. The whole room was silent, so still he could hear noises outside from the storm kicking up. Sure September weather for this part of New Mexico.

But he didn't have to say a word.

Ash jumped up off the sofa and stalked out of the room, showing her distaste for her brothers' announcement.

Seemed like a good decision. Jace followed Ash, and with a last annoyed glance toward his brothers, Galen departed the meeting, too.

They had nothing more to talk about.

ASH CAUGHT UP TO FALCON as he saddled his horse. "Wait, Falcon."

He turned, not in the mood for conversation. "A storm's coming in. I've got things to do."

She gazed up at him. "I am so sorry. About everything."

"Don't be. It's not your fault."

His sister put a hand on his arm. "Falcon, I hate seeing you miserable."

He smiled, but even he felt the unintended sardonic angle to it. "I'm not miserable." He was something else he couldn't define, and the only description that was coming to mind was *in love.*

If this was love, it truly did stink.

"You just need to talk to Taylor," Ash said.

"Funny, but I think I've had all of your advice I need, sis." He mounted his horse, the one thing on this planet he trusted at the moment, and settled his hat on his head. "I'm going to ride Xav's shift in the canyons. Keep him in the old bunkhouse closest to the house until he's healed. Under no circumstances is he to go back to his post until he's completely well, and even then, not until the shooter is found. If he argues, tell him that we don't have enough insurance to cover him getting killed."

Ash's face paled in the light from the barn's overhead lamps. "You can't go out there, Falcon."

"Who can? You?" Falcon shook his head. "You shouldn't have been out there in the first place. You let your emotions get the best of you. I don't intend to make that mistake."

He urged his horse out of the barn into the darkness, and once clear of the fence surrounding the house, took off at a gallop he hoped would chase some of the pain away. *If* you could ride off pain, cleanse your soul of it by putting miles between you and your devils.

But Falcon knew he couldn't. The devils were lodged firmly inside his heart.

TAYLOR DECIDED SHE WASN'T going to wait any longer for Falcon to make an appearance. It was the beginning of December, and she hadn't seen Mr. Marry-Me since September.

"Big chicken," she muttered.

She collared Ash and Fiona stringing white Christmas lights along the corrals, creating the traditional fairyland look of Rancho Diablo.

"Hi, Taylor," Ash said. "Coming to join the party?"

"Grab a ball of lights," Fiona said. "We're happy to conscript anybody and everybody into the Christmas spirit. How's your mother, by the way?"

Taylor shook her head. "I'm going to have to pass on the decorating, though I'd love to help another time. And Mom's fine, thank you. She's talking about taking a trip, which I never thought I'd hear her say. But she's feeling so much better she wants out of the house." She took a deep breath. "I'm looking for Falcon. Do you know where I might find him?"

Ash gave her a strange look. "We don't see him much. Maybe once a month, if that."

"Once a month?"

"He's become a bit elusive," Fiona said. "He took over Xav's post after Xav got shot. Won't give it up. Xav, of course, can't be housebound—" she glanced at Ash, who blushed "—so he's gone to work at Dark Diablo in Tempest."

Taylor blinked. "So Falcon's in the canyons?"

Ash nodded. "Haven't you heard from him?"

"Not a word." And she was going to yell his ears off when she finally did see him. Mr. December-I-Do, indeed.

"Oh, dear," Fiona said. "We figured if he was keeping in touch with anyone, it was you."

"Why me?" Falcon was the biggest snake that had ever slithered. Boy, did she have a shocker for him.

"Well, because of the proposal," Fiona said, and Ash turned back to the lights she'd been stringing, but not before Taylor caught the expression on her face.

Guilt.

"Is there something you'd like to add to that, Ash?" Taylor asked.

"Um…" Ash fiddled with some lights for a moment, then turned to face her. "I think if you want to talk to my brother, you're going to have to go find him."

"She can't go into the canyons by herself," Fiona said. "Galen will freak out. There'll be all kinds of fussing and cussing if Galen finds out either of you have gone there again, after what happened to Xav, and especially now that we're shorthanded."

"Shorthanded?" Taylor waited to hear the rest.

"Tighe and Dante deserted us," Ash said. "My brothers are traitors, not to put too fine a point on it."

"Can I borrow a vehicle?" Taylor asked. "I wouldn't ask, but mine won't make it out there."

"Certainly." Fiona bustled off to get the keys, and Ash looked at her, her expression worried.

"Taylor, I hope you know that I want you and Falcon to work things out between you," Ash said.

"You mean since you told your brother about my date in September, and he sent Tighe and Dante to spy on me?" Taylor crossed her arms. "I haven't seen Falcon since. You mean that kind of work things out?"

"I didn't think Falcon would take it that way. He's always been such a knucklehead, but that was more knuckly than usual."

Taylor shook her head. "I'm sure you meant well."

"I did!"

Ash's face was so earnest Taylor felt herself relent just a bit.

"Here are the keys," Fiona said brightly. "Head due north. I hope you can find him. He's elusive, I'll grant him that. Even Jace can't find him at times, and he can track anything."

"Not as well as me," Ash said. "I could find him, if my stupid brothers would let me go look. No one's as good at sniffing people out."

Taylor took the keys. "Thanks, Fiona."

"There's a small-caliber pistol I put on the passenger seat, just in case. The snow's coming, so don't be long, please," Fiona said, concerned. "I'm pretty sure I'll get my ears yelled off by Galen for letting you go, so if you could be back before nighttime—"

"I will."

"Good luck," Ash said. "I'd come with you for backup but I'm on a tight leash thanks to overprotective, bossy brothers. And we're shorthanded around here, like we said."

"It's a fifteen-minute drive. I'll be fine. Thanks."

Taylor got in the military jeep, noting the basket of cookies and thermos of hot cocoa Fiona had tucked into the passenger side. Hidden underneath a warm, fuzzy blanket was the pistol. Everything necessary in case of an emergency.

Now she just needed to find Falcon. That was the real emergency.

Chapter Eight

Living in the endless gorges and canyons near the breathtaking mesas that framed Rancho Diablo had taught Falcon a lot. He'd survived the barren spirit-breaker that was Afghanistan, and now here he was, in his own backyard, surviving once again.

Surviving until December. Waiting the whole damn thing out. What else could he do?

It was cold now, and had been since the beginning of November. The first crisp winds had blown in the middle of October, wrapping him in a chilly embrace he welcomed. With each snowfall, each test to his well-honed survival instincts, Falcon felt stronger.

Some would say he was hiding, but no man could hide from himself forever. He'd dealt with his raw emotions where Taylor was concerned, looked into that mirror of jealousy and confronted the longing he didn't want to feel.

Yes, he was stronger.

The grasp of the crush he'd had on Taylor had become clear to him. Jillian had been right—Taylor would never be happy with him. She deserved a well-off man, someone unscarred, a more genteel sort. He was too hard-bitten and rough-edged to make Diablo's best girl happy.

Wisdom had not been easy to accept, but the gracious thing about wisdom was that it was patient, waiting for you to mature into acceptance of its erudition.

So he had. And felt like a healed man.

He sat on his horse, eyeing the stretch of snow-crusted land between him and Rancho Diablo, surprised that he felt a strange sense of homesickness. Perhaps just before Christmas he'd return and test his heart's readiness to face Taylor again.

A jeep roared toward him, leaving wide tracks in the snow. It was almost as if he'd conjured her, because he could see the long chocolate of her hair in the distance. Of course, it couldn't be Taylor—no one at Rancho Diablo would send her out here alone in a jeep. So it was a mirage, like the Diablos, a mirage of his longing.

Maybe he wasn't as healed as he'd imagined.

She pulled up beside his horse and switched off the jeep. He couldn't speak for the shock of seeing the object of his dreams materialize so unexpectedly.

"Hi, Falcon," she said, and it was the same sweet musical voice he remembered so well.

Well, he wasn't dreaming. Hadn't gone mad from endless hours of envisioning her on her seemingly endless quest for a better man.

"What are you doing here?" he asked, his voice rough from lack of use. It surprised him that his words came out so gruffly, but Taylor didn't seem fazed.

"Obviously, I've come to see you." She got out of the jeep and picked up a basket, which she handed to him. "This is from Fiona. Comforts from home."

He blinked. "Uh, I'll put that on the table in my kitchen."

"Okay, smart aleck." She put the basket back into the jeep. "I'm pretty sure she meant for us to have something to snack on while we chat, but if you're going to be a boor, we'll go with that."

"What are you doing here?" he repeated, unable to get past the fact that Taylor had shown up in the middle of nowhere.

"It's December," Taylor said, "and I believe you proposed to me. By the way you're hiding out, I can only assume you're reneging on your offer."

"Okay," he said. "Now that we've got that settled, you should head back before the storm rolls in."

She looked at the sky. "Storm?"

He shrugged. "I'm figuring on a good six inches of snow. Thanks for the eats, but it would be safer if you went home."

Sending Taylor away was the last thing he wanted, but he was operating from the new well of wisdom he possessed. Better not to allow wily temptation to rule his newly acquired, hard-won knowledge.

She looked at him with impatience. "Look, cowboy. Let's just quit dancing around the subject matter and get everything straight between us, because it wasn't easy for me to come out here and find your boneheaded self. No woman goes running after a man who makes love to her and then never darkens her door again, in fact, hides from her, so this is the only time I intend to throw myself out here like this. Fair warning."

A little panic banged on his heart as he dismounted from his horse to face her. He tried to remind himself how much he cared about this woman, but he pushed the panic away ruthlessly, not about to get caught up in his emotions again. Otherwise the three months he'd spent out here alone with his thoughts and his heartache were going to be for naught—all the good wisdom that had been finally knocked into his superthick skull wasted. "I think things are best left as they are."

"You're officially reneging on your proposal?"

He nodded. "Yes, ma'am."

"All right." She took a deep breath, stepped close to him. Looked in his eyes, seared him with her deliberate stare. She poked a finger in his chest, and he'd never wanted to grab her and kiss her senseless as badly as he did at this moment. "Listen to me, you big chicken, you weasel of epic proportions. I wouldn't marry you if you were the last man on earth."

Thankfully, she hadn't come to tell him she'd picked another bachelor and was ducking out of the so-called agreement. That had been his greatest fear when she'd pulled up in the jeep. The relief was practically blinding.

"Okay," he said, smelling sweet perfume and maybe some peach shampoo. His mouth dried out with longing. "I accept that."

"You will accept that, you louse, because I'm not giving you a choice." Her eyes flashed at him. "I'm having a baby, and the last thing I'd ever do is to marry a chickenhearted weasel who's scared to death of his own feelings."

Falcon felt as if a boulder from the canyons had fallen on him. He could barely breathe. "A baby? My baby?"

She slapped him, not hard enough to make his ears ring, but enough to bring him clarity. "Sorry," he said. "I don't know why I said that."

"Because you're an idiot," Taylor said crisply. "And a louse."

He blinked, recognizing that he was caught between the proverbial rock and a hard place, with a mad female not prepared to give quarter. Falcon shook his head, then laughed. "Holy smokes, I'm going to be a father."

"Yes, you are." She turned to walk away, but he caught her arm.

"Don't go off in a huff," he said. "Since you've gone to the trouble to come all the way out here, stay and share Fiona's basket with me."

"I don't think so." She pulled away and stared at him, greatly annoyed. "I shouldn't be surprised that even your condoms weren't trustworthy, courtesy of the bearer."

He laughed again, delighted with her spunk, thrilled at the news that he was going to be a dad. "Boy or girl?"

She sniffed. "I'm not telling you. I don't want you involved with my pregnancy at all."

He pulled her to him, crushing her against his chest, smiling. "You little devil. You left me out here all these months suffering, and you knew you had the ace."

"I have no idea what you're babbling about, but it sounds like a lot of Callahan doublespeak to me," she muttered against his chest. But she didn't pull away, so Falcon took the liberty of stroking her long dark hair, enjoying the silkiness of it. God, he'd missed her.

"Does my family know?"

"Just you, you boob. I didn't want any of them rushing out here to tell you. I figured they'd send up smoke signals to give the news if they had to, and then you'd probably run as far as Maine to get away from me."

He couldn't help the grin on his face. "I'm so glad you came out here to ask me to marry you."

She pulled away, her face wreathed in annoyance. "I did no such thing. I wouldn't ask you to marry me if you were the last man on earth."

"So you said."

"Just making sure you're listening, cowboy." She went to the jeep, got the basket out, set it in the snow. "There's your Christmas cheer. See you next year."

She got in the jeep. He let her go, the grin on his face stretching from side to side. Oh, he'd let her run, for now. Work off some of that womanly aggravation she was wrapped in so righteously.

But she'd better work it off quick, because he didn't intend to wait very long to make sweet, thorough love to her.

He'd waited long enough.

"HERE SHE COMES!" Ash and Fiona scrambled away from the spot where they'd practically been camped, keeping an eye out for Taylor's return. The two of them had been worried sick that Galen or one of the others would ask where the jeep was before Taylor returned. Or if she didn't return—and they had to confess what they'd done. "Get back to stringing lights, pretend like we weren't spying on her, and let's never do that again!"

"It was your idea," Fiona said. "If you hadn't meddled in the first place, if you hadn't egged your brother to go to Tempest to strut his stuff in front of her date, Falcon would still be on the ranch and they'd still be on speaking terms that don't last just twenty minutes! In the future, you leave the meddling to the pros."

Ash unwound a spool of lights so fast she could

barely concentrate. "It's your fault for keeping us all working against each other for a ranch. We're the only family whose aunt deliberately stirs the sibling rivalry."

"If you've got it, flaunt it, I always say. Now pipe down," Fiona said under her breath. "Act merry!"

The jeep engine switched off, and Ash and Fiona arranged their faces into pleasant, nonconspiratorial expressions.

"Did you have a nice drive?" Fiona asked, with a trace too much sugar, Ash thought.

"Yes, thank you. I appreciate you letting me use the jeep." Taylor handed the keys back.

"No basket?" Ash asked, trying not to blurt out the obvious question she really wanted to ask—*Did you find my hammy-brained brother?*

"I left it." Taylor's expression didn't seem as happy as it should. "Merry Christmas, if I don't see you ladies again before the holidays."

Taylor got in her own car, while Fiona and Ash gaped after her.

"Stop gawking," Fiona said. "Wave and act like our curiosity isn't killing us."

They waved and smiled, Callahan manners on display.

"That did not go well," Ash said.

"Not a bit," Fiona agreed.

They waved harder, smiles stretched wide and friendly.

"Whew," Fiona said, when Taylor's car had disappeared from sight. "It's exhausting being an aunt!"

Ash looked at the Christmas lights that had yet to be strung along the fence. "We overplayed this."

"Too late to do anything about it now. We're going to

have to let nature take its course. Never an easy thing, because nature can be quixotic." Fiona sighed. "Two stubborn hearts trying to work out the excesses of love is hard on the spectators."

"Oh, brother," Ash said. "Do me a favor, don't do my love life any favors, okay?"

Fiona adjusted her blue gloves, settled her blue wool cap over her white curls. "I wasn't aware you had a love life, niece," she said, too sweetly.

The sweetness had the barb of truth in it.

"You know what I mean. No assistance from the peanut gallery, if and when I ever catch my cowboy."

"You just remember you didn't want my help," Fiona said, giving her a jaundiced glance that spoke volumes.

A slight shiver washed over Ash, a vague reminder that a smart woman didn't toss an aunt's charms and blessings to the wind lightly. Maybe she'd been too harsh. A touch ungrateful. They all benefited from Fiona's love and tutelage, even if sometimes her "guidance" could come under the heading of well-meaning, shazam!-style destruction. A veritable poof-cloud of mayhem could be wrought in an instant by Fiona's capable fingers. Still, no *irreparable* harm was ever done— mostly. Ash glanced at Fiona's sweet, doughy face, but her aunt was deep in her own thoughts.

Ash went back to arranging lights, thinking that a white Christmas wedding was what was needed to bring some cheer to this depressing joint and her dispirited aunt—but it looked as if Christmas gloom was setting in fast instead.

"READY OR NOT, here I come," Falcon said, settling his horse in the barn and grabbing his truck keys. He'd given his little mama-to-be a week—plenty of time to get over her pique, which he hoped was long enough to let a woman's ire subside.

"Hey," Ash said, appearing at his elbow. "Where're you off to?"

He looked at his sprite of a sister. "Thought I'd run over to…someplace."

No point in mentioning his mission. Too many cooks in the kitchen had already severely impacted the recipe. And he was trying to be a gentleman, no easy feat when he wanted to rush over to Taylor's and sweep her off her feet.

He and Taylor had a lot to discuss. She'd been oh-so-cute shifting all the blame on him about an unlucky condom—but she knew quite well that when the condoms had run out thanks to a certain sexy lady, she'd whispered sweetly that it wasn't that fertile time of the month anyway, and then seduced him out of his good sense.

Oh, Taylor knew very well what had happened that night, and he'd let her slide on the detail. Because it didn't matter in the long run how they'd become parents, they were going to be parents, and he couldn't be happier.

But it was time to get the curious clan out of their business.

"Well, if you're planning to go see Taylor, she's not there," Ash said.

"How do you know?"

"She and her mom left about five days ago." Ash gazed at him with sympathy. "I didn't know if you wanted to know or not, and I'm on a new mind-my-own-business mission."

"You should do that. Be good for you," Falcon said, his mind spinning. "Where'd they go?"

"I just said I'm minding my own business," Ash said, "and you said I should. Wild horses couldn't drag any further information out me." She stalked off in a little-sister huff, and Falcon quickly realized he'd erred.

"Wait a minute." He followed Ash. "You can mind your business all you want, but I need to know where Taylor's gone."

She looked at him. "Don't you have her cell phone number? Ask her yourself. If she wants you to know, she'll tell you."

"Of course I don't have her cell phone number." Falcon frowned. "Do you?"

Ash sighed. "That also falls under the heading of mind-my-own-business, if I had it, which I'm not saying I do. Falcon, I'm done meddling. Don't ask me any more than I've told you. Why don't you have your girlfriend's phone number if you proposed to her?"

He sighed. "She wasn't my girlfriend."

"You asked her to marry you." Ash stared at him. "But you didn't ask her for her phone number. It's almost embarrassing."

"I'll figure it out." He went off, telling himself that pinching his sister's head off wasn't appropriate. Ash was right about one thing: he shouldn't have let Taylor get away. He'd been trying to play it too cool. Things would have gone more smoothly if he'd been his old domineering, alpha wolf self. Hot and demanding instead of cool and laid-back.

"Last time I let people throw me off my game," he muttered, and went to find Fiona.

"Look what the cat dragged in," his aunt said brightly

when he entered the kitchen. "Just in time to help me hang wreaths."

"Ah," he said, about to decline. Then he realized that the fastest way into Fiona's heart—and therefore her phone book and her gossip hotline—was to hang wreaths. "Let's get to hanging, then."

She looked at him. "Did you hear about Taylor?"

This was going to be easier than he thought. "Hear what?"

"She's getting married," Fiona said, and Falcon rolled his eyes. The Diablo grapevine was the fastest in New Mexico, but it was moving at a turtle's pace now.

"Yeah, she's getting married. To me."

Fiona blinked. "Not to you, silly. She's marrying Benton H. Withers III. She said you took back your proposal and so she chose one of the three bachelor princes, and that happened to be Benton H. Withers III. I like saying that. It sounds so regal. The Third. Ha, ha, ha."

Falcon shook his head at his aunt's laughter. "The hell she is. She's marrying Falcon Chacon Callahan the First. Go ahead and spread that all over the grapevine, Aunt, because I'm not about to give my baby to another man to raise, nor my woman to another man to love."

"Baby!" Fiona exclaimed. "A baby! When did that happen?"

But he didn't have time to talk. He left the kitchen, heading to find his sister, who *was* going to tell him everything she knew this time—and then he was going to track his little baby mama down, if he had to go to the four corners of the earth to find her.

And drag her to the *nearest* altar.

Chapter Nine

Taylor had told Benton she needed this one last trip with her mother before wedding bells rang, and it had nothing to do with the nervous feeling that had hit her ever since she'd accepted Benton's proposal.

He'd been okay about the baby, and thrilled that she'd agreed to marry him. In fact, if she wasn't in love with Falcon, Benton would be a wonderful choice for a husband. Unfortunately, Falcon had completely ruined her for other men.

Which had been his intention all along. In spite of her misgivings and Jillian's warnings, she'd fallen for him, irreparably and completely.

It had hurt so much when he'd said he was reneging on his proposal. "He really was a cad," she said out loud without meaning to, as she drove her mother through Texas on the way to Florida, trailing a refurbished silver Airstream trailer they'd rented from a local dealer.

"Probably not a cad," Mary protested. "He didn't know about the baby."

"He's still a proposal-reneging cad. But I should have expected that."

"I don't know why," her mother said. "You didn't give him time to get over the shock, honey."

She hadn't. But she'd wanted Falcon to say he still wanted to marry her—before she told him about the baby. Then it wouldn't feel so much like she'd stacked the deck to keep him. Once he'd said he didn't want to marry her, well, wild horses couldn't have dragged her to an altar where he was standing. "Let's change the subject," she said, catching sight of a dark truck in her rearview mirror. "Let's talk about Florida."

"I can't wait to see those white sands," her mother said with a happy sigh. "I've waited years for this."

"I know. It's going to be fun." And then she'd marry Benton, and forever be Mrs. Withers, and... She eyed the truck more carefully. If she didn't know better, she'd think the gold Callahan *C*s were painted on the truck, but it was impossible to tell for certain. Why would a Callahan truck be in Texas? They weren't close to Hell's Colony, where she knew a bunch of them resided. "We're going to sit on the beach and stare at the ocean and—"

"You can sit. I'm going parasailing," her mother said. "I laid in that bed long enough that I don't want to do any sitting. I want to see the sky."

Taylor laughed. "We'll do it."

The truck pulled up on their passenger side.

"Look! It's Falcon Callahan!" Mary exclaimed. "He's waving. I think he wants us to pull over."

Nerves attacked Taylor like a cloud of mosquitoes. She carefully maneuvered the truck and Airstream onto a long lane at the next exit.

"It's so romantic!" her mother said. "Don't you think?"

"I don't know what I think, other than I think he's

crazy," Taylor muttered. "At least this will give us a chance to stretch our legs."

Her mother laughed. "I assume Falcon's here for more than exercise and a turn in the fresh air."

"I've agreed to marry Benton, and that's what I'm going to do," Taylor said with determination.

"If you love him." Mary looked eagerly out the window. "My, he is a handsome drink of water, isn't he?"

Yes, he was. While she agreed with her mother's comment, there was no reason to egg her on. Taylor got out, went around to help her mom out of the truck, but Falcon beat her to it.

"Hello, Mrs. Waters," he said, just like Beaver Cleaver, Taylor thought sourly. "Hi, Taylor."

"Falcon, what are you doing here?" she demanded.

"I've come to talk you out of your course of action," Falcon said, and Taylor said, "You have a problem with Florida?"

Mary drifted away after patting him on the arm.

"I have a problem with you marrying another man," Falcon said, "when you should be marrying me. I'm trying to save you from yourself, as it were."

"Is that so?" Taylor gazed at him and crossed her arms. Darn it, he was sexy and confident, and it all just made her mad. All those months he hadn't so much as called, and now he wanted to upend her life.

Just when she'd gotten over him.

Mostly.

Well, maybe not so much. She was crazy mad for him. But she'd already been down that road once, and at the end of it was heartache. "Thanks, Falcon, but I'm good with saving myself. I saved myself when you weren't around, and I'm pretty happy with marrying Benton."

"You're happy with it?" He cocked an ironic brow. "Sounds like you're buying a car."

She flattened her lips, annoyed. "Butt out, Falcon. That's the most polite way I know how to put it."

He sighed. "Darling, you really don't have to fight this hard. You know I make you happy in a way old Benton never will be able to."

She felt herself blush. Okay, she'd considered the fact that she wasn't all that attracted to Benton, not at all, actually. It wasn't going to be a marriage of fire-and-ice like it would most likely be with Falcon. Passion was going to have to be sacrificed for common sense.

"I'm not going to discuss this with you anymore."

He frowned. "Are you marrying him just because you're having my baby?"

She walked away a bit farther so she could keep an eye on her mother. Mary had gone into the Airstream and pulled out a lawn chair and a cold drink. She looked happy enjoying the December day. It was much warmer in Texas than when they'd left New Mexico, and Mary couldn't wait for the hot weather in Florida. The virus and resulting side symptoms she'd had for six months had kept her so housebound that Taylor thought her mother might become a permanent sun-seeker.

Taylor turned to face Falcon. "I'm marrying him because I want to."

"If it's about a name for our baby, you know the only name he should wear is Chacon Callahan."

That was the sticking point Taylor could never get past. So in the end she'd made a different decision. "I'm moving to New York with Benton."

Falcon shook his head, then shrugged. "All right. If you've made up your mind, I won't try to change it."

"I have." Taylor nodded vigorously, eager to convince herself and Falcon, too.

"Then there's nothing I can do." Falcon tipped his hat to her, backed up, putting space between them. "Thank you for hearing me out."

"You're welcome." He wasn't. She felt completely dissatisfied, as if he'd just given her permission she didn't need, to do what she'd been perfectly satisfied with not ten minutes ago.

With Falcon standing in front of her, staring down at her with navy eyes and long dark hair and a gently confused smile, Taylor didn't feel satisfied at all.

She felt as if she was making the mistake of a lifetime.

But there was no way to get out of said mistake gracefully. He'd forever know that he could just snap his fingers and she'd give up everything to be with him, which was exactly what she wanted to do more than anything.

That didn't seem wise. She'd been so hurt when he'd taken back his marriage proposal.

"I know this is just about the baby, and the ranch," Taylor said softly. "Trust me, I'm making the best decision for both of us."

"You let me think for myself, little lady, and I'll let you think for you." He tipped his hat again, went over to say goodbye to Mary. Taylor waited, giving the two of them a chance to chat. After a moment, Mary got up, threw her arms around Falcon's neck. He seemed pleased by the attention.

"Guess what, Taylor?" Mary exclaimed. "Falcon's agreed to drive us to Florida!"

Taylor's gaze jumped to Falcon, who shrugged as if he was pure as the driven snow.

"Doesn't that sound like fun?" Mary put up her chair with a content smile. "I always say three is the perfect number for traveling!"

Taylor had never heard her mother say any such thing. Falcon winked at her, and Taylor was pretty certain he hadn't heard such a point of view before, either.

This was her mother's trip. If Mary wanted Falcon along, then fine.

But if her mother was trying to pull a Fiona-style ambush, it wasn't going to work.

"THIS IS SO EXCITING!" Mary said, as Falcon and Taylor took her to the gate at the Houston airport the next day. Falcon had slept in his truck at the state park, and her mother and she slept in the Airstream.

Which apparently had given Falcon time to think of a plan that required just a tweak or two to suit his purposes.

"I said I wanted to see the sky, and this is even better than I hoped!" She leaned up to kiss Falcon on the cheek. "Thank you so much for the airplane ticket. I'll be sure our rooms at the hotel are just right!"

Falcon smiled, and Taylor shook her head. This was a plan no doubt cooked up between the two of them.

Taylor knew she'd been outmaneuvered, Callahan-style.

She hugged her mother goodbye. "I'll see you in a couple of days. Enjoy the extra fun time on the beach."

Her mother gave her a tight squeeze. "I'm going to enjoy every second!"

Taylor smiled. "I thought you said three was the perfect number for traveling."

"I can count," Mary said. "You, Falcon and your baby make a perfect three. Toodles!"

Her mother went through Security, beaming, waving goodbye as she went off on her adventure. Taylor turned to Falcon.

He held up his hands in mock surrender. "I had nothing to do with it. She said she felt riding in the truck so far was tough on her, and she was going to buy her own crack-of-dawn ticket."

Taylor walked out into the bright Texas sunshine. "And the first-class plane ticket, and the fancy hotel rooms? We'd been planning on staying at a state park in the trailer."

"Well," Falcon said, and his voice was a tad too innocent, "I had frequent-flier miles and hotel points. Does it matter? Your mother deserves a nice vacation. She's been through a lot."

It was so true. Taylor couldn't argue the point, and secretly thought it was sweet that Falcon would do such a nice thing for her mother—even if he was being a bit sneaky about his intentions. Her mom would love having a dream vacation, and being pampered.

"I think you know my mother probably thinks she was being Fiona-like by trapping us together for a couple of days," Taylor said. "It's not going to work."

"No, I seriously believe that bouncing on the truck shocks was hard on her body," Falcon said. "I take her at her word."

Taylor climbed behind the wheel of her vehicle. "Falcon, you had Galen pick up your truck, but you can take a plane back to New Mexico, you know. We're right here at the airport." She looked across at him. "I can drive to Florida by myself."

"Believe me, I plan to let you." He pulled his hat down over his eyes. "This is a vacation for me, too. Drive, chauffeur."

She drove from the airport and eased onto the highway. "Last chance to catch a flight home. At least until probably New Orleans."

"I'm fine, darling. You just quit your chatting and let this cowboy rest."

His phone buzzed, and Falcon pulled it out to peer at it, then shoved his hat back down over his eyes. "I hope you don't mind, but I made hotel reservations in New Orleans. Let me know if you need me to drive."

Taylor felt steam begin to come out of her ears. "I do not need you to drive, and what is wrong with staying at a state park?"

"I have goals," Falcon said. "I was deployed for a few years, then went almost straight to working at Rancho Diablo, which, nice as it is, isn't exactly a vacation. In fact, it's sometimes a bit stressful."

Stress the Callahans sometimes caused themselves, Taylor thought. It was because they were so arrogant and pigheaded. "What does that have to do with goals?"

"I've never stayed in a Ritz. Seems like something I should do, doesn't it?"

Taylor blinked. "A Ritz Carlton?" She wouldn't be able to pay for such a thing. She and her mother lived on her earnings from Banger's, and some of her mother's retirement income, though they tried not to touch that.

"My hotel is on wheels right behind this truck. It's not deluxe, but it's fine for me."

"Still," Falcon said, "my baby says he'd prefer the Ritz."

"Uh-uh," Taylor said. "If I'm having a boy—and I'm still not telling you what the sex is—he's a tough guy. He'll take the trailer. And I know what you're trying to do."

"What?" He was too casual.

"You're trying to compete with Benton."

Falcon laughed out loud. "Okay, you got me."

She hadn't figured he'd admit it.

"Is there anything wrong with that?" Falcon asked.

"Yes. There is. It's unnecessary."

"Maybe, but I've always wanted to stay at a Ritz. It sounds very different from caves and mountains in Afghanistan. Not that it was always bad," he mused. "But I'm looking forward to sleeping on feather pillows."

Taylor straightened. "Falcon, what hotel do you have my mother staying at?"

"Well," Falcon said, "her flight lands in Fort Lauderdale, where she will stay at the Ritz for two nights. Then she's flying out to stay at some swanky place in Bermuda, connecting from Atlanta. It was a little bit of going around her elbow to get to her wrist, but your mother's dying to check out the best beaches." He looked at her. "Didn't she tell you her plans?"

Taylor counted to ten. Tried to rein in her temper. "Falcon, this isn't going to work."

"Why isn't it?"

"You can't just take over my trip with my mother."

"It's December," Falcon said. "I figure I've got fifteen more days of romancing coming to me, and romancing is what I intend to do. Can't blame a guy for sticking to the plan, can you?"

She wanted to yell at him, she really did. She wanted to be angry.

The problem was, she was flattered he was trying so hard. If he was trying to win her heart, he might be succeeding.

FALCON STUDIED the driving directions on his phone, and then the map in his lap. Taylor still wouldn't let him drive, wouldn't relinquish any control. Had refused to eat dinner with him last night, keeping him at arm's length, warding off romance. He'd gotten a king bed, of course, but she'd ordered her own room, as if he were a prickly cactus she didn't want to get too near.

Sometimes it was best to let a woman have her space. It didn't matter, because he was less than two feet away from Taylor. He fully intended to show up ol' Benton, and as long as he was in Taylor's truck, he felt he was ahead of the game.

But if she intended to ignore him all the way to Florida, he was going to have to shake her out of her comfort zone.

At the next stop, Falcon and Taylor went inside for a lunch snack. She called her mother, smiling as she got off the phone.

"She's having a wonderful time. Says everybody's treating her like a queen. Never had so much fun on a vacation." Taylor's face glowed with happiness. "Thank you, Falcon."

"Happy to do it for my future mother-in-law. What?" he asked, keeping his face innocent.

"I'm marrying Benton," she said, as they went back

out to the truck. "You don't believe me, but we'll both be happier this way."

"Okay," he said, not worried about ol' Benton. Tighe and Dante had reported that Benton was a fingertip-kisser, a slow-gamer. They'd instructed him not to play a gentleman's game, and though his brothers could be goofballs, he figured this was good advice. Good guys won only if they generated heat. Lots of sexy heat.

"I'll drive," he offered.

"I'm good, thanks." She got in, turned the key.

The engine didn't start. Didn't even crank. Falcon looked out the window, completely unfazed.

He heard her try again, and then again.

"It won't start," Taylor said.

"Maybe it's the heat," Falcon said. "You had the truck checked over before you left Diablo, right?"

"Of course." She tried again. "Nothing."

"Huh. Odd." Any more comment than that and she might be suspicious. He let his lasso out slowly to keep her from spooking.

"Maybe you could look under the hood."

He smiled at her. "I could, but I know zip about mechanics."

"Nothing?"

"Sorry."

She sighed. "I guess I'll call roadside assistance."

"That sounds like a good idea." He looked out the window, peeked back over at Taylor, noted the sweet roundness of her stomach where his son resided. "Or," he said, "maybe we don't wait for three hours for roadside assistance to come and figure out the problem, and *possibly* fix it today. Could be longer than three hours, depending on the problem. Could be a couple of days."

"Days! My mother will be in Bermuda by then!"

He shrugged. "We could leave it here while they repair it, and fly to meet your mother."

"I—" She looked around. "You think that would be best?"

He nodded. "Definitely. More fun, too."

"Okay," she said reluctantly. "I think you're right."

"Good." He didn't mention he'd already bought tickets on his phone. While she called roadside assistance and dug her suitcase out of the back of the Airstream, he finished making arrangements for his brothers to come and get the Waterses' vehicles.

They wouldn't be needing them. When he and Taylor returned from their vacation, it would be on a plane, and they would be married.

This was their pre-honeymoon, even if Taylor didn't think that was what she wanted. It was up to him to show her what she did want—*him*.

Chapter Ten

"How's the snare?" Ash asked Falcon, having finally caught her brother between sudden urgent phone calls he was sending to Rancho Diablo. He needed backup—someone to pick up his not-bride-to-be's vehicles. Which meant she was probably going to get pressed into duty soon.

Her brother owed her. Big-time. She should never have told him where Taylor was going. Why couldn't she keep her big mouth shut.

"What snare?" Falcon demanded.

"The one you're trying to set for Taylor."

"Is 'snare' what the ladies are calling marriage these days?"

Ash sighed. Her boneheaded brother would have to figure out his love life on his own, if he could. "Hey, I need a favor. Because you owe me, and all that."

"Name it."

"I want you to tell Xav he has to come back to Rancho Diablo. I don't care what the reason is, just send him back here."

"That's cheating, isn't it? Using his job with the family to force him near you?"

"*Cheating*'s a harsh word. I prefer to call it *encouraging*."

Falcon laughed. "I can't do that."

"And I shouldn't have told you where Taylor was." Ash looked out the kitchen window of Rancho Diablo, noting the three inches of snow piled up on the ground. "Are you going to be home for Christmas?"

"Not sure. Going to ride this ride as long as I can."

She shook her head. "Tell Xav we're short on coverage. It won't be a lie."

"Ash, look. If I send him back to Rancho Diablo, he'll just go hide in the canyons again. He's afraid of you."

"Afraid?" She frowned. "Why?"

"I don't know why men are afraid of women. They just are. I think he's a little scarred from watching his brothers and sister give up their freedom." Falcon was silent for a moment. "Hey, Ash, have you ever thought that maybe you want a different guy? Maybe Xav isn't the one."

She gasped. "Fancy support coming from a man whose intended bride has had two proposals in the last ninety days. How would you feel if I told you that even though you somehow got Taylor pregnant, perhaps she was destined for someone else?" She bit a nail, thinking. "Actually, she's been texting me to hunt up a wedding gown for her. She thinks that since we've had so many brides around Diablo, perhaps someone knows of a gown they'd like to sell. It's not a bad idea, especially since two of the Callahan sisters-in-law own the bridal shop in town."

"Wait," Falcon said, "back up. What two proposals did Taylor get?"

"One from Benton and one from Storm Cash," Ash

said. "Which is really dumb, because she turned Storm down right off the bat, and then he asked me out to the December ball. Personally, I think Storm is lonely."

"I don't care if he is," Falcon said. "I have to go, sis. We're about to board."

Ash straightened. "About Xav—"

"No." Falcon's voice was a little rough. "If a man is interested, nothing can stop him from being with the woman he wants, Ash. Xav's not interested."

The phone clicked off. Ash turned off her phone, sank onto a kitchen chair. Of course. Falcon was right. Xav wasn't hiding from his feelings—he was hiding from her.

And she'd practically chased him away.

It was a very bitter thing to accept, but Ash knew it was true.

She went to find Fiona, her heart stunned and sore.

Fiona was curled up on a sofa in the sunroom, a box of tissues and some steaming tea beside her. "Hi," she said, her voice croaky.

"You're no better?" Ash sat down next to her aunt.

"It's just a stupid cold trying to slow me down. Luckily, I have this new gadget," she said, showing Ash her laptop, "because I'm ordering Christmas presents like mad. Thankfully, Santa delivers by mail when necessary."

Santa didn't deliver all dreams by mail. Ash sighed. "Aunt Fiona, we have to talk. Are you up to it?"

Fiona closed her laptop eagerly. "I always feel like talking."

"It's come to my attention that I'm wasting time—"

"Mooning after a certain cowboy," Fiona said, her

eyes bright. "I heard some of your conversation. Sorry about that."

"It's all right." Ash looked at her aunt. "I hate those women who throw themselves at men."

"Oh, honey, don't worry about throwing yourself. You only want a man who can catch you when you launch yourself his way."

"I think he doesn't," Ash said, a trifle sadly.

"Then pooh on him. I'll have the roof advertisement changed for you instead of Taylor. Goodness knows, we raked in the calls from possible princes. There are more men looking for a good woman than ladies realize."

"It's you, Aunt Fiona. You just always figure out the proper lure." Although it wasn't working for Falcon, either.

"It's packaging," Fiona said, looking her over carefully. "We'll package you differently than we did Taylor, of course, and the bachelors will come running!"

Ash shook her head. "That's the thing, Aunt Fiona. I think I want something different."

Fiona blew her nose, popped in a cherry-flavored cough drop. "Tell your fairy godmother."

Ash smiled. "Aunt Fiona, I don't really think you have a wand."

Fiona looked startled. "What do you mean?"

"Just that I'm too old to believe in Santa Claus and fairy godmothers."

"Well, that's a sour way to live." Fiona sniffled. "Goodness me. Don't let Xav suck all the romance out of you."

"My life has been about reality. Reality works for me." Ash looked at her aunt, realizing how much she'd come to love her over the past year they'd all been at

Rancho Diablo. "Aunt Fiona, I know you don't have a ranch for us to win."

Fiona's eyes went wide. "Could you repeat that, please?"

"I know you don't have a ranch for me and my brothers to win." Ash felt almost bad, as if it was Fiona's bubble that was being burst rather than hers. But it was time for everyone to face the facts.

Fiona shook her head. "Ash Callahan, I'm surprised at you." She gave her a shrewd look. "So what is it that you think you want now, since you haven't got a man or a ranch to work for? No prizes left to win, so to speak?"

"I think I need to find my place," Ash said softly. "I think I want to leave Rancho Diablo."

FALCON COULDN'T REMEMBER when he'd been more stunned. He hung up his phone, turned to look at the woman who was carrying his child. Storm Cash had proposed to Taylor? Why?

He couldn't wrap his mind around that. The whole thing with Benton he did understand. Taylor thought Falcon didn't want to marry her—he'd told her that—so she'd looked to greener pastures for a name for her baby. Benton H. Withers III was no threat to Falcon.

But Storm? That was his family's enemy. He couldn't understand how that relationship could possibly have come about. He stared across at Taylor as she sat reading a magazine, realizing he didn't know her as well as he'd thought. She'd never once mentioned another proposal, and certainly not from Storm Cash.

He flung himself into the seat next to her. "So that was Ash on the phone."

Taylor looked at him. "Oh?"

"Yeah. Your trailer's made it back already. Turns out it was a simple fix on the truck." Very simple. He'd just disconnected the battery.

Maybe he was getting karmic payback.

"So, Ash mentioned that Storm Cash had proposed to you." He hadn't meant to blurt it out, but it was killing him.

"Oh." Taylor went back to reading her magazine. "Yes, he did."

Annoyance smote Falcon. "I wasn't aware you knew Storm that well."

"He's nice enough. I can't say I know him well." She didn't look up from her reading. "He said he knew things had been tough for Mama and me, and he wanted to help us out."

Falcon doubted Storm did things just to help out. Irritated tickles ran along the back of Falcon's neck. The man just bugged him in the worst way. "I wish you'd told me."

She looked at him, surprised. "Why? What difference does it make?"

It made a lot of difference. "Just didn't realize you'd had two proposals in the last few months."

"Three," Taylor said, "if you include yourself, which I really don't."

Well, that was just nice, Falcon thought. She didn't count his proposal. He shook his head, thinking.

He'd never considered himself a quitter. He was a fighter, like the rest of his clan.

But this was Diablo's best girl, and everybody knew it, and marriage proposals weren't an uncommon occurrence in her life. Nothing he'd done had made a difference—except getting her pregnant, and that was the thing that was keeping them together. And apart.

Falcon couldn't stop the wild hammering of his heart. He closed his eyes, went inside himself, tried to stop the sensation that his world was falling, exploding.

"Are you all right?"

He wasn't certain. "Maybe it's a little hard for me to know that my marriage proposal is lumped with Storm's."

"Lumped how?"

"You…me. I'm not any different than Storm to you."

"Falcon, I never went out with Storm."

"You never went out with me, either."

She looked at him. "We went out. You took me ghost-busting. I shot off the toe of a boot for you, buster. Your uncle's friend complained that I took off his toe, but he exaggerated." Taylor looked annoyed. "We did have a date, Falcon. I never went out with Storm."

He wasn't happy. "Storm is no friend of my family."

"He comes into the diner from time to time." She went back to reading her magazine. "I can't call him a friend, but I don't think he's a boogeyman, either."

She couldn't understand. She didn't know Rancho Diablo's history. Falcon looked at the mother of his child, feeling very low. He'd never considered the possibility that Taylor didn't dig him at all. That night he'd made love to her, she'd certainly seemed like she dug him—a lot—but ladies were fickle, weren't they?

That was the hard part of being a guy. You just never knew what they were really thinking.

"Ash shouldn't have told you," Taylor said.

"Why? Why didn't *you* tell me?"

"I didn't tell you Benton had proposed, either," Taylor said. "And you didn't tell me you'd discombobulated my truck."

He wanted to kiss her madly. She looked at him with those bright eyes and that soft smile, and he really thought that if he could just get her alone, in a romantic place with no Rancho Diablo, no brothers, no sister and no wily aunt, he could convince her the best way he knew how that she belonged with him. "Ash tell you about the truck?"

"Mmm." Taylor put her magazine away. "It's time to board. You coming? Or chickening out?"

She picked up her small bag and got in line. How had she known he was developing an extreme case of cold feet? That fear was washing over him like waves on a beach?

He couldn't resist a challenge—and she'd just thrown one down he couldn't walk away from. She knew that, too.

But he was still highly bugged about Storm. She probably knew that as well.

He followed Taylor onto the plane.

FIVE HOURS LATER, Taylor was on the beach, staring out at the ocean, and trying not to ogle the cowboy next to her. Okay, she totally hadn't factored in the sight of Falcon in nothing but trunks. Black trunks that showed off a lot of muscles and a well-toned body. Women up and down the beach stared as they walked by, and when Falcon walked to the ocean to get on a surfboard he'd rented, ladies sat up to watch.

It was annoying. Taylor felt ungainly in her solemn

black pregnancy tankini, not sexy at all. And ever since Falcon had found out about Storm, he'd been a bit quiet, maybe even distant. Very silent, for him, which was new.

It was almost as if he was going through the motions of being with her now. Which was a very strange change, since he'd been in hot pursuit up until he'd found out about Storm. He'd almost convinced her that he really wanted to marry her, despite the fact he'd said he no longer wanted to.

Frankly, he was the most confusing man she'd ever met.

Not that she had a whole lot to compare him to.

He flopped down in the chair beside her, bringing a bit of the ocean with him. All the women beside them lay back down, and Taylor considered the wet, muscled cowboy next to her. "Mom called."

"Oh?"

The firm, rippling body just about had her sidetracked. She remembered too well how hot Falcon could make her. She tried to focus on her agenda. "She said she's flying off to Turks and Caicos."

He rolled over to stare at Taylor. "I had nothing to do with that."

"This time."

"That's right. This time it's all on Mom." He looked confused. "What's in Turks and Caicos?"

"Apparently," Taylor said, "Mom met a rich guy who wants her to travel with him. She has a passport, she has some money you apparently gave her—"

He held up a hand. "Just enough to cover some expenses and a little extra. Not enough money to find a fortune hunter, if that's what you're implying."

Taylor giggled. "Mom wouldn't go off with a fortune hunter. He paid for her ticket and hotel. Turned out to be someone she knew from high school. If I didn't know better, I'd think there was a Callahan behind that fix-up, but I really believe it was just a chance meeting."

"Good." He rolled back over.

"So now there's no need for us to go to Bermuda," Taylor said.

"Guess not."

Taylor studied his wide brown shoulders, the lightning-strike tattoo on his right one—apparently, all the Chacon Callahans wore the same tattoo, but she didn't know what it meant—the lean waist, and wet, dark hair streaming against his neck. "So we should go back to Diablo."

"Yeah."

He'd gotten himself in a right twist over the whole silly matter with Storm, and she had no idea how long it would take for him to work it out of his system. She wasn't quite engaged to Benton, but she had told him she'd think about it—and she wasn't thinking about Benton at all because all she did was drool over Falcon.

And drool she did.

"Sometimes it's hard for me to look at you and realize you're the father of my child."

He rolled over, put his arm behind his head. "It's harder for me to look at you and realize you're the mother of my only child."

She sneaked another look. Yep, still hotter than any man had a right to be. "Why?"

"It just is." He sighed. "It was a bad idea for me to

shanghai you into this trip. Sometimes I have a problem with boundaries."

He sounded as if he regretted their time together. That bothered her more than she'd expected it would. "I should be mad at you. I was, in the beginning."

"Was?"

"Well, I wish you'd asked." She looked at the long stretch of brown skin next to her. "Then I realized I was having fun, so I got over it. But you have to ask in the future. No more Fiona-style traps."

"Fine. And you have to tell me if you consider any more proposals," he said gruffly. "It's getting hard to keep score."

"Remember when Jillian told me that you were too wild for me?"

"I remember," he said. "You didn't have to put the shoe on the other foot with such enthusiasm. I'm beginning to get an inferiority complex."

Taylor smiled. "I very much doubt that."

"Look what I had to do to get you on this trip with me. I've bribed people from New Mexico to Florida. You didn't have to take Jillian's advice so much to heart."

Taylor shook her head, not about to encourage his beefing.

He raised up on his elbows to look at her. "I vote you give ol' Benton a pass. He'll never be able to keep up with you."

"For your information," Taylor said, "and not to give you any sense of satisfaction at all, but I already told 'ol' Benton' that I couldn't accept his proposal."

"That's exactly as it should be." Falcon put his arms behind his head, lounging with satisfaction. "I've knocked out two men with proposals. That means mine's gonna stick. Three's the charm."

She patted a sun hat onto her head. "Whatever you have to tell yourself."

"So, when's the big day?"

"What big day?" With Falcon, there could be any number of big days.

"The day my son arrives."

Taylor took a deep breath. She couldn't keep him in the dark any longer—he'd worked so hard to try to get in her good graces. And it was working. Bit by bit, she found herself trusting Falcon more and more—and falling more and more. "Baby Emma Marie Joy will rock your world in May."

"Baby Emma Marie Joy?" He sat up. "We're having a girl?"

She nodded.

He let out a whoop and tugged her from her chair, crushing her to him. Over his shoulder, Taylor could see all the bathing suits that had admired his surfing foray in the water sit up, staring over at them. Falcon laughed out loud. "I'm having a little girl!" he yelled, and all the bathing suits looked disappointed, although they clapped before they lay back down on their chairs and towels.

Taylor smiled. "Let go of me, Falcon."

"I don't think so. I'm celebrating. We're celebrating." His voice caught a little, grew husky. "I want Emma to know her father was the proudest dad on the planet. And that her mom looked sexy in her bathing suit when she finally gave me the good news." He stroked her ponytail, and after a moment, Taylor relaxed and leaned against his chest. They lay on the sand like that until the sun went down, and Taylor thought it was almost perfect.

Almost.

Chapter Eleven

Falcon got up the next morning, his whole world bright. In the next room lay the woman he'd been trying to catch for months, pregnant with his daughter. He grinned, stretched, punched the air. Life was getting better all the time.

If he could just get Taylor to the altar.

"At least I ran off ol' Benton." He packed his suitcase, got ready to check out. Last night had stretched long without Taylor. He hadn't tried to entice her into his room, and so he'd lain awake, his mind racing, too excited to sleep. Somehow he had to convince Taylor that a Christmas wedding was an absolute necessity. He didn't want his daughter ever thinking her father had been a slacker.

Taylor could be stubborn, though, in the same league as Fiona and Ash. Wrangling her to the altar would take skill, finesse. A sure, patient hand.

"I'm in over my head," he muttered. He was much more the get-the-job-done kind of guy, and that approach wasn't going to work with Diablo's best girl.

He picked up his suitcase, went to find his little woman. She didn't answer when he knocked. Checking his watch, he tried not to be concerned. Their flight left in a couple of hours; they should be on their way to the airport.

Maybe she was downstairs eating breakfast. "My daughter was probably hungry," he said proudly. Callahans were good eaters, and Emma would likely follow the family tradition. He went down to find Taylor, and when he couldn't, he headed over to the desk.

"Mrs. Callahan took the early flight back, Mr. Callahan," the desk clerk said, and Falcon was so stunned, he didn't even notice the Mrs. Callahan bit.

"The early flight?"

"Yes, sir. She said she had a change in plans."

"Thank you." Falcon slunk back to the room to get his suitcase. That little devil! He knew exactly what she was up to: she hadn't wanted to return with him. The whole town of Diablo would have been agog with gossip at them returning together. He hadn't thought about it, but no one knew he'd joined Taylor and her mom on their trip.

"That little devil," he muttered. "She gave me the slip."

It was a week until Christmas. All he wanted for Christmas was a bride, his bride.

She was harder to catch than a shooting star.

He was going to have to figure out a way to do it.

Two days before Christmas, Falcon still hadn't figured out how he was going to settle his footloose lady.

"Romance isn't for lightweights," Ash said. "It's really more for tough guys."

He didn't point out that his sister's face was longer than a shadow. "Still haven't heard from Xav?"

"Stay on you, brother. I can handle my issue. My love interest isn't having a baby."

Still, her face was glum, despite her brave words. Falcon saddled his horse and pondered his dumb luck. "According to Jillian, Taylor says she needs time away from all men. So she went to stay with friends up north. Since her mom is still traveling, and seems pretty captivated by her new beau, Taylor told Jillian she's free as a bird. Leaving me here like an unkissed toad," he groused.

"Poor thing." Ash got up, tightened the stirrups opposite the side he was on. "That's what you get for jumping the gun."

"What gun?"

"The one that says the man is supposed to win his woman, then get her to have his child. Taylor was always afraid your interest was just in the baby. Because of the ranch, you see."

"Whatever. I'm sick of hearing about that land. I just want Taylor to marry me." He sighed. "I threw everything I had at her. I wined her, dined her, whispered the sweetest of nothings—"

"Yes, so now you're just going to have to wait."

He hated the sound of that. "Wait?"

"For her to make up her mind."

"Wait for her to toss me into the trash heap like Benton?" He did not belong in this limbo. "Haven't you got better advice than simply wait?"

"Nope," Ash said, wandering off. "You'll just have to develop patience, something no Callahan has in abundance."

Didn't he know it. "My sister, the font of impossible knowledge."

But maybe he had a source he hadn't yet tapped. He rode into Diablo, threw the reins over a post, went into the Books'n'Bingo Society tearoom and bookshop.

Nadine Waters beamed at him. "Falcon! How nice to see you!"

"Thank you. It's good to see you, too."

Her eyes sparkled. "I bet you've come to ask about my niece."

He laughed. "Not to put it too plainly, yes."

She waved him to a seat, took a chair across from him. "I have no good advice where Taylor's concerned. She's always been our girl who makes up her own mind."

"Yes, ma'am." He just felt so out of sorts. Surely love was easier than worrying about scorpions in the desert.

Then again, maybe not.

"She won't be back for Christmas?"

Nadine shook her head. "I'm afraid not. Can I get you some tea? Some cookies?"

"I've already got them," Corinne Abernathy said, setting a floral teacup and a tiny dish of cookies down next to him. "Hello, Falcon."

"Hi, Falcon." Maxine Night sat, too, her gaze sympathetic. "We hear you've got quite the situation on your hands."

"Yes," Corinne said, "but how lovely that you're going to be a father. No doubt your daughter will be just as plucky as her mother!"

"I can almost count on that," Falcon said, brightening just a bit. "The thing is, though, I'd rather have two plucky ladies in my house, if you know what I mean."

They nodded eagerly. He picked up a cookie to encourage them. "Maybe you could tell me where Taylor went?"

The three women shook their heads solemnly.

"We've been sworn to ultimate secrecy," Nadine said. "Taylor says she needs time. And you know what it means when a woman says she needs time, don't you?"

He sighed. "It means I'd better give it to her. Or I'm toast."

"Maybe not toast," Maxine said, "but definitely not the happiest loaf in the bread box."

That was that, then. There was nothing he could do. His woman had played the Time card, and now he'd have to suck it up and wait.

"But," Corinne said, her tone bright, "the good news is she spoke favorably of you before she left."

"She did?" He perked up.

"Yes. My niece said that if she was ever going to choose a man, it would have been you."

Falcon felt a surge of hope. "If?"

"Well," Corinne said, "remember, you offered her a proposal on the spur of the moment. Taylor never quite trusted that you knew your own feelings."

"She could have asked," he groused.

"But then there was the baby," Maxine explained. "Every man wants a baby."

"Not really," Falcon said, thinking about his lunkhead brothers, Tighe and Dante. He couldn't see either of them with children. They were children themselves. Babies, really. "This stinks to high heaven."

The ladies looked distressed. He could tell they honestly were trying to help. "Sorry," he muttered.

"It's all right," they quickly said, their tones comforting.

"We understand completely," Nadine said. "You just have to believe in love, Falcon."

He got up, thanked them for their advice and their hospitality, then slunk off to his horse and rode slowly toward home, his heart heavy.

As he went past the window of Banger's, Falcon never saw the shadow of a man move into place behind him, watching his every move.

"BROTHER'S GOT TO PULL his head out," Galen said to Fiona, and Ash nodded in agreement. "I've never seen a man as low as Falcon. He has no concentration whatsoever."

"Best to leave him alone," Fiona said, but Galen shook his head.

"It's another hole in coverage. He's not able to focus on anything but his own misery."

"Don't sell him short," Ash said. "He's focused *here,* unlike Dante and Tighe." She frowned. "And let's not let Jace off the hook. Ever since Dante and Tighe, the resident Casanovas, retreated, Jace has been chasing down the nanny bodyguards with the complete joy of a man who has the field wide-open."

Fiona shook her head. "I don't know what to do. The wheels have just come off around here."

"Which means we're due a strike of some kind." Galen looked worried. "We may have to bring in backup until things settle down. By the way, it's good to see you feeling better, Fiona."

"Yes. That cold I had was a doozy."

Ash thought their aunt still looked a bit peaked. "Are you sure you're feeling better?"

"I'll be well enough by Christmas. Have to get Burke

to play Santa. I can't wait to go to Hell's Colony and see all the children again! It's been quiet around here for too long. Gets on my last nerve."

She went off, humming a Christmas carol.

Ash looked at Galen. "Is she pushing herself?"

"A little. Her aura's a bit off. She'll come around." He pondered his sister for a moment. "We need more help around here."

"You could talk to Xav."

He nodded. "He'd come back if we asked. Xav knows what we're facing here."

Ash sat up. "You really think he'd come back?"

"Sure. Nobody rides the canyons quite like he does."

Her blood chilled as she thought about someone shooting Xav. Nothing had showed up on the casing; there was no match to a bullet purchase. But someone had shot him, and if she hadn't found him, he might have died.

"No," Ash said. "I'll take the canyons."

"I don't want you down there. We'll send Jace."

Jace's brain was like a pinwheel these days. On his day off, he chased Ana and River. "Not Jace. It has to be me."

"I'll do it." Falcon walked in, and Ash shook her head vehemently.

"Absolutely not. You're going to be a father in May. You have to get Taylor to marry you. Your plate is full."

"I agree with Galen. You don't belong in the canyons," he argued.

Ash stood. "Yeah, well. Guess what? I'm a better tracker and a better shaman than all of you. I'll be fine." Besides, the cold loneliness would take her mind off Xav, which she needed.

She stalked out, her mind made up.

Falcon looked at Galen. "So stubborn."

"Yes, and she's right." His brother sighed. "She is better than all of us. I just don't like my little sister being out in the elements."

"We'll lock her in the basement."

Galen laughed. "Good luck with that." He studied Falcon. "Any luck with the runaway fiancée?"

"I'm counting on the Christmas spirit to work its magic on her."

"And then?"

Falcon went to the door. "I'm going to tell Ash I'm taking the canyons. I've got nothing better to do with my life than wait on something that may never happen."

Galen frowned. "Don't say that. Stay strong."

"I'm strong. I'm just outgunned in the stubborn department." Nadine and Company had told him he was going to have to be patient. No better place to be patient than endless, freezing canyons under gray winter skies.

Falcon left and went to find his sister, who would no doubt open up a can of sass on him. He'd had lots of experience with it lately. "I'm becoming immune to sass—that's the good news."

It was his only news.

"FALCON CAN'T DO CANYON shift," Taylor protested.

"He's such a pain in my butt," Ash said. "He insisted. I even tried to hypnotize him but he laughed and told me not to be such a newb. I did not appreciate that."

Taylor looked out the window of her tiny house in Key West. It was so warm here it was hard to imagine the cold in Diablo. But it would be cold there, and snowy, and she hated the thought of Falcon exposed to the elements—and the danger.

"It's no big deal," Ash said. "Falcon's been in colder, much worse places. I just thought you'd want to know you won't be able to reach him. There's no cell service out there, and I didn't want you to worry."

Taylor was worried. "I can't help it. But I can't make his decisions for him."

"Yeah, I know. But if you came home, he'd come back to the ranch, and then I could go ride canyon. He's being an overprotective ass. I'm much better equipped to handle what's out there, and he's going to be a dad. He should be buying baby booties and reading up on how to make organic baby food or something."

Ash sounded disgusted. Taylor smiled. "I'm not getting in the middle of a family quibble. Sibling rivalry is something I have no familiarity with. I'm an only child, remember."

"Yeah, but you don't want Emma to be an only child," Ash said, her tone a little sneaky and maybe a bit hopeful. "I just think if you come back, Falcon would settle down a little. He's been wild as a coyote lately."

Taylor shook her head. "I'll think about it. But I'm not making any promises. I don't want to rush anything with your brother, Ash. Falcon wasn't interested in marrying me until he found out about the baby. It just doesn't feel right to me to force a relationship."

"Okay. I get that. I don't like it, but I get it. Hey, I gotta go. Fiona just went by, and I think she's got a plate of fresh gingerbread. Take care of my niece, Taylor."

Taylor hung up and thought for a minute, and then she punched some numbers into her phone.

"This is Falcon."

"Falcon, it's Taylor."

"Where are you?" He sounded just like he always did, demanding, in control.

"I'm staying out of the cold." She looked out the window at the row of small gingerbread houses on her street. Tiny flowerpots decorated some porches; others had latticed windows. Getting away for a while had been good for her, and maybe Falcon, too. "I hear you're taking over Xav's ride."

"Yeah. Might as well. I've got nothing better to do. Unless you're coming back?"

She took a moment. "Actually, I'm not."

"I'd like to spend Christmas with you."

"I just wanted to tell you to be safe," Taylor said, sidestepping the holiday talk. The last thing she wanted to do was let Christmas spirit force either of them into something they didn't feel.

"I don't want to be safe," Falcon said. "I want to do something really dangerous. I want to marry you. It's the most dangerous thing I can think of. What do you say?"

Taylor closed her eyes. "Let me think about it."

He didn't love her. She knew he didn't. "You know," Taylor said, "the statistics on marriages that are started because of a baby aren't good."

"I don't believe in statistics," Falcon said. "That always sounded like so much voodoo to me."

"It's good to talk to you, Falcon. Stay safe."

Taylor hung up, feeling terribly unsettled. Maybe she was making a mistake. Her mother was having a renaissance, enjoying her new beau. Mary had thrown caution to the wind and was having the time of her life.

Six months ago, no one would have thought she would be able to get out of bed.

The first second she could, she went on a major life adventure.

"What am I afraid of?" Taylor murmured to herself, but she knew. She knew marriages that started impetuously probably didn't last.

For Emma's sake, she needed this one to last. There were no guarantees in life. None.

She went to pack her suitcase.

Chapter Twelve

Falcon sat straight, deep in thought in the stone ring, in front of a very small fire—not a large enough fire to be easily seen, and yet he had no desire to hide. He knew they were out there, and they knew he was here. To him it really didn't matter.

It was Christmas Eve, and he was meditating. Far away from family, he went inside himself to make order of the chaos he felt. He had a thousand questions and no answers.

Kind of a lonely Christmas, but he'd rather be here than odd man out in Hell's Colony. Or suffering through the cheery sights and smells Fiona would have spun all over Rancho Diablo.

Much better to be here, alone with his private thoughts, and yes, his misery. He wouldn't be good company.

He heard the sound of an engine in the darkness, and then the engine turn off. Without opening his eyes, he listened to footsteps coming toward him. His visitor wasn't bothering to disguise his presence. Ash walked a bit lighter; he wouldn't have been totally surprised if his sister had taken a bit of pity on her big brother and brought him some Christmas dinner or something. It would have meant braving Galen's wrath, but Ash had been known to go against their eldest brother's wishes.

His visitor wasn't any of his brothers, either. They moved like military men, with a bit more stealth.

This visitor wasn't cautious. Falcon heard boots on the gritty snow, purposeful footsteps. Not Fiona, not Burke and not Grandfather. Any of them would make a different type of approach.

Not Wolf. He wasn't so careless, usually. Wolf was sneaky. Falcon and his brothers had been warned about Uncle Wolf even when they were children.

"Darn it, Falcon," he heard a voice say, and his eyes snapped open. He leaped to his feet, crunching over the snow to greet the mother of his child.

"What are you doing here?" he demanded.

Taylor shone a flashlight his way. "I had this strange idea that we should spend Christmas Eve together, you goob. But if you're going to be all growly, I'll go hang out with Aunt Nadine's family."

He was so stunned to see Taylor he barely knew what to say. In the flashlight beam he could see her rounded stomach. She looked wonderful. Her chocolate hair was long and had a piece of silvery tinsel strung in a barrette. She wore a long, red corduroy dress and boots. Her gloves and knitted cap with the sparkly bow on top gave her a look that was downright festive. "You're the last person I expected to see."

"Is that a good or bad thing?"

He pulled her to him, drinking in her warmth and the smell of sweet perfume he associated with Taylor. "You're always a good thing."

"I brought hot chocolate and Christmas cookies.

And some marshmallows if you're in the mood to roast them."

He just wanted to kiss her. He couldn't, of course; she had to set the pace. But she was here and that was all that mattered. "I've got the fire."

"Fiona said you would. In fact, Fiona even sent along a long-handled pan of popping corn she says is organic." Taylor thought for a moment. "Is organic corn better for you?"

"I don't ask. I just eat whatever my illustrious aunt puts on my plate."

Taylor went to unload the jeep, handing him the long-handled pan. "Supposedly this is antique. Your aunt says you'll love it. You have to keep shaking it gently over the fire, but she swears there's nothing more romantic than staring at the stars and popping popcorn over an open fire. I thought it would be too noisy, but Fiona says even Wolf has to take a night off for Christmas Eve."

Falcon wasn't so certain. But it wouldn't matter. If Taylor wanted romance, he was all for making it happen.

"Of course," Taylor said, carrying a wicker basket as she followed him, "I told her romance wasn't on the list. But it sounds like fun, so I brought the pan."

Maybe she wasn't looking for romance, but he was. There was always a chance the Christmas spirit could change Taylor's mind, right?

He spread a blanket on top of the waterproof sheet he'd put under his sleeping bag near the fire, so she could sit more comfortably. "I don't think you should be out here long," he said, his voice thick with emotion. "It's too chilly. I don't want you or little Emma catching a cold."

Taylor sat on the blanket and watched him put the pan over the fire. "I won't get cold. I'm bundled up with so many layers I can barely feel the chill."

If he had his way, she wouldn't feel any chill at all. Falcon shook the pan lightly, and popcorn began to explode. He hadn't smelled popcorn in so long he couldn't remember the last time he had.

"You know, Fiona's right. This is fun," Taylor said. "The stars are beautiful."

He grunted. "Why are you here, anyway?"

"I told you. I wanted to spend Christmas Eve with you."

Was she bringing bad news to him? About to tell him that she'd changed her mind about ol' Benton and was going to marry him?

"I've been thinking about you, and me, and Emma," Taylor said.

He brought the popped corn over, sat next to her. "And?"

"I think," Taylor said, "it would be best for Emma if we spent a little more time together."

"Sounds good to me." He didn't say more, didn't want to rush her. Yet hope was beginning to sneak cautiously into him.

"I feel as if clearing up communication between us would help us later on with raising our daughter."

He couldn't take it. "How much more time?"

"Whatever we decide." She shrugged, took some of the popcorn. "This is good. Fiona's always right, isn't she?"

"Not really. She let you come out here in the darkness without an escort, and for that, I should be plenty mad at her. I'm just so happy to see you that I'm not mad like I should be."

"I have an escort," Taylor said.

"Messrs. Smith and Wesson?"

"Them, and your sister followed me halfway out here. She's gone now. She's going with Burke and Fiona to Hell's Colony. There'll be nobody but me at the Rancho Diablo house." Taylor sighed. "I'm only allowed to stay here with you for an hour. Fiona says I have to call her immediately on the hour, or she's phoning up the sheriff and the National Guard."

"That's better. At least she has some sense of caution." He knew his aunt. She was more concerned about matchmaking than safety. "I didn't think I'd see you before the New Year, if then."

"I wasn't planning on coming. But then I heard that you were down here, and I came to lodge a complaint. I don't want what happened to Xav to happen to you."

"That was a fluke. Xav thinks he just got a little careless and someone got a shot off. I'm never careless. In fact, I'd probably see them before they'd see me."

"I don't like it," Taylor said, sounding tense.

"Hey, you're not actually worried about me, are you?"

Taylor shook her head. "Of course not, not excessively. Eat your popcorn."

"Not excessively?" He laughed. "What does that mean?"

"It means of course I'm worried, but not to the point that I lose sleep over it." She sniffed. "Much, anyway."

"You're cute when you fib," Falcon said, suddenly getting it. "You *have* been worrying about me!"

"So?" She glared at him, pushed the popcorn away, popped open a water bottle and sipped. "Emma would be disappointed if I didn't worry about her father a little bit."

"Emma, is it?" He smiled to himself. "What did you really come out here for?"

"To raise your blood pressure." She leaned against his shoulder, and they looked up at the stars together. "I figured it was time for us to share this journey. Once I heard you'd taken canyon duty, I knew you needed me at your back."

He moved her off his shoulder so he could stare down at her. "You're not serious."

"Sure I am. Of course I am. What wife leaves the father of her child to face danger alone?"

"A smart wife." He shook his head at her. "If you're thinking you're going to stay out here with me, you're not."

"We either share our lives or we don't."

"And if we don't?"

"Then what's the point?"

He touched her nose, then her lips, then spread his hand over her stomach. "I think we have bigger fish to fry at the moment. Emma belongs in a comfortable house. Not out in the open where—"

"So I'm just supposed to be the silent little woman who sits at home while her man is out protecting the world?"

"What would you do if I was still in the military? You couldn't follow me to Afghanistan." He smiled. "Much as I'd want you to be around."

"And that's the point. You're not in the military anymore. You and I can be together. Otherwise it wouldn't be a marriage. There's just no way two people who don't know each other very well grow into a marriage when they don't share their lives."

"We're not married," he said, and Taylor said, "Well, I'm trying to marry you."

His eyes widened. She loved the look of surprise on his face. "What are you saying, Taylor?"

"It's Christmas. You waited, just like Jillian suggested." She smiled, enjoying his suspense. "I always thought a Christmas wedding would be lovely."

"Are you serious?" He sat up straight.

"Callahan, tying you down is what I want for Christmas," Taylor said.

"But I don't want you out here," Falcon said. "That's the catch, isn't it? You want to be a warrior wife?"

"I want to be with my husband. There's the big bunkhouse nearby and the ranch isn't far."

He shook his head. "There isn't a man alive on this planet that would allow his wife to be out in the elements where known mercenaries are."

She got up, began loading the jeep with the popcorn pan and the basket. "Well, we're going to have to compromise somewhere. I'm not going to just sit in the house and wait for Wolf to send me a ransom note for you."

"That's what you're supposed to do!"

Taylor looked at him. "Two heads are better than one. I'm a good shot, and you know it."

"You're having my baby! Babies need to be safe inside a house."

"Was Ash safe inside a house?"

"We're not talking about Ash," Falcon said, but Taylor got in the jeep.

"Merry Christmas, Falcon. I have to get back or Fiona will send the sheriff. Or your grandfather, which is the equivalent of a platoon of soldiers. She worries."

"*I* worry. I don't get any respect for worrying." He got up in the jeep next to her. "I'm following you back."

She smiled. "You can't. Your brothers will say I've ruined your focus."

He leaned over, kissed her. "Are you sure about getting married?"

"If you compromise a little about us being apart. I just think we can't let your uncle Wolf ruin our marriage from the start. There's a million little things that can go wrong in a marriage. A good one takes work. How can we work on it if we're apart?" She kissed him back, lingering just a little, drawing out the moment, teasing him with her lips.

"You're trying to seduce me into seeing your side."

"Is it working?"

"It just might be. Let me get my horse. We'll discuss this more in front of a warm fireplace."

She looked around at the frosty darkness. "What about your post?"

"Everybody's about to ship out. That leaves only me and you. I imagine you can bend my ear a little better when your teeth aren't chattering."

She smiled. "See you at the house."

He got out of the jeep, went to the stone circle to pack up his things. Falcon couldn't really understand that she was too afraid of him getting shot, the way Xav had. Maybe Falcon wouldn't be as fortunate as Xav had been.

She wasn't able to sit up in the warm, cozy house, waiting for something to happen. Ugly images stirred her mind; she remembered the night Falcon had been jumped by his uncle and his companions. What might have happened if she hadn't been there? Would Wolf have harmed his nephew?

She'd always known the risks of getting involved with a Callahan. But that didn't mean she couldn't help even out the risks.

FALCON LET HIMSELF INTO the house that night, locked the door behind him and went looking for Taylor. She was waiting by the fireplace, where a roaring fire backlit her sweet face.

"So this is Christmas Eve," Falcon said.

"Yes, it is." She got up to pour him a cup of mulled cider. "Merry Christmas."

"You're scaring me," Falcon said, and he meant it. She really was, on so many levels. "I think you're serious."

She smiled, touched her mug to his. "I've never been more serious."

"You're romancing me because of Emma."

"Can you think of a better reason?"

"No." Glancing around, he saw no signs of family. All the Christmas presents were gone from under the tree, except one. "Fiona and everyone headed to Hell's Colony?"

Taylor nodded, cute in her black velour jogging pants and jacket. "The sleigh left."

A knock at the kitchen door halted what he was about to say. "Expecting someone?"

Taylor got up and followed him. "Mom's still traveling with her beau and Fiona didn't want me far away from where she felt like she could keep tabs on me. No one else knows I'm here."

Falcon opened the door. Frigid air blew in, swirling around them. He stepped outside to look around, and waved Taylor back, his suspicions suddenly gone haywire. He'd definitely heard a knock—Taylor had heard it, too.

He went back in, locked the door behind him. Went back to the fireplace. "Taylor?"

There was no answer. Falcon's blood chilled. He waited, then checked the bedrooms and the halls. By the Christmas tree, the lone gift sat, its foil wrapping colored by the twinkling lights. The mugs of mulled cider remained in front of the fire.

Closing his eyes, Falcon concentrated, listening. His heart beat so loudly it was hard to hear—but then the fire popped, sending up a shower of sparks, and he felt the hunch, the warning, that had saved his life on so many occasions.

He checked his gun, moved to the front door—a door that was rarely used at Rancho Diablo because everybody always used the kitchen door, even friends who came to call. He went out, scanned the dark landscape, saw the footprints in the snow, scraped and disturbed, signs of a struggle.

Of course. It made so much sense.

They would know tracks in the snow were a stark giveaway. Wolf didn't care, was flaunting his control. He'd taken Falcon's woman and child. Falcon was without backup.

He started tracking the bootprints away from the house.

TAYLOR WOKE UP slightly disoriented. She looked around the room, tried to rise from the bed she was in. The room was small but clean. Sparse. Tan walls, wood-beam ceiling, a wooden rocking chair in the corner. No rug on the floor, just rustic dark hardwood.

She got up, looked out the small window. Two feet of snow smoothed the landscape. There were tall green trees, though, which weren't part of Rancho Diablo's beautiful surroundings.

She wasn't in Diablo anymore.

She went to the door, tried the knob. Locked.

"Hey!" Taylor banged hard on the panel. "Hey!"

A moment later, the door opened. "I know you," Taylor said to the woman who entered. "You were with Wolf the night he took Falcon."

The brunette shrugged. "What do you want?"

"I want to know where I am. And why you've taken me."

"You're in Montana. The why is pretty obvious, don't you think?"

Taylor blinked. "Montana?"

The woman nodded. "Do you like your room?"

"I don't care about the room. Why did Wolf take me?"

"I'll let him tell you his plans. My job is to keep you quiet."

"I don't do quiet very well." Taylor was mad. "You know Falcon will find me."

The tall brunette smiled. "Well, we certainly left enough bread crumbs for him to follow."

"Oh, I get it. I'm just the decoy. Wolf's out to finish what he started before."

"Only you don't have a firearm this time." Her captor went to the door. "Do you need anything?"

"Yes. A gun. And bullets."

"I don't think so." She smiled sardonically and went out. Taylor heard the door lock. Sinking down in the rocking chair, Taylor ran a hand over her stomach. "Don't worry, Emma. Your daddy's smarter than your great-uncle."

After a moment, Taylor got up and looked out the window. So they were using her as a lure to get to Falcon. Wolf was determined that Falcon knew something or possessed something he wanted.

Wolf knew Falcon would come for her. They had just spoken of marriage in front of the fire and Christmas tree at Rancho Diablo. Falcon would come for her and Emma, and Taylor hated that she was the bait for the trap.

There was nothing she could do but wait for the right moment to act.

THE TEMPERATURE ON Christmas morning at 4:00 a.m. was twenty-two degrees Fahrenheit. Stringy gray clouds draped a moon valiantly trying to light a dark night. Falcon followed Taylor's tracks—there were three sets of footprints—to a cave where a small fire had been doused. Recent signs of occupancy littered the cave: bones from a small animal that had been roasted over the fire, some cigarette butts, a cracker package.

But the cave was clearly abandoned now.

Taylor had been here, though. He could see her boot marks, the heels dug into the snow. Her captors hadn't troubled to mask their path, and Falcon knew they expected—wanted—him to follow her.

"She was here," his grandfather said, walking into the cave. Running Bear stood tall and lean, his face stern with shadows. "They knew she is the closest thing to your heart."

That was true. Falcon knew what he had to ask, as much as he hated it. But the question had bothered him for a long time. He looked at Running Bear. "Am I the hunted one you spoke of?" he asked, his voice a sharp rasp.

His grandfather shrugged. "Only the spirits know. You have to be on guard no matter what. No one can say the who or what of it, just that these things come to pass."

"I don't understand. And I need to find Taylor." *And my daughter,* came the cry from his heart. No one, not even his grandfather, could understand Falcon's anguish. Taylor had said in the beginning that she wasn't sure she wanted to get involved with a Callahan and their history.

She had good reason to feel that way. And now his legacy had been visited on her and his child.

"You can't find her," Running Bear said, and Falcon stared at his grandfather, stunned.

"Can't?"

"Will not. You have to let her go."

"Let her go? I'm not going to let her go. She's going to be my wife. She's having my child. I—"

"Love her. I know this. *They* know that." His grandfather squatted near the cold fire pit, studying the ashes. "Until your child is born, you will not find her."

Falcon blinked. He felt an overwhelming desire to shout in frustration, but instead calmly squatted near his grandfather. "Our child isn't being born until May.

I need to rescue Taylor *now*. They can't be that far off. And they left tracks a first grader could follow."

His grandfather nodded. "It's a trap."

"I'm prepared for traps."

"So are they."

He didn't understand. "What is it they want from me?"

"If they can take you, they'll use you against your family. They'll use you to get to your parents, and Molly and Jeremiah Callahan."

"What difference does it make now? Our parents have been in witness protection for too many years for anything that happened before to matter."

"When a drug cartel is destroyed, the memories are long. The Callahans are still here. Until they are gone, the drug routes cannot be reopened. Traffickers can't use this entire area. The Callahans keep too sharp an eye out, and they built up the city of Diablo. Now too many people are watching for the enemy."

Falcon waited with a sinking heart, knowing his grandfather wasn't finished.

"In the old days, when the smugglers nearly had the run of the land, Jeremiah Callahan made a decision to stay and fight them. He wanted to see the town of Diablo built up and thriving for families. It was his way or the smugglers' way, and the battle was fierce. He and Molly made a good team. The town trusted them, believed in them. Jeremiah understood the land, understood the strength of spirit for a people. Your father, Carlos, believed his brother's cause was worth the fight, and he and your mother had connections to the government that they used to inform on the cartel. When the smugglers went down, the Callahans made longtime enemies. No, they have not forgotten. You do not know because you did not live it, so the understanding is not in your heart yet. But it will be."

"Why does Uncle Wolf want to bring his brothers down?"

"Because Jeremiah and Carlos are of the sky, and Wolf is of dark wind. Wolf made a deal with the cartel that if he would turn over his family, all of Rancho Diablo will be his."

"The land," Falcon said. "The tribe owns the mineral rights, correct?"

"True, but the land and the buildings are enough of a prize. Never forget that the Diablos are Wolf's main goal. All men wish to tame the spirits. It cannot happen, but Wolf is a creature who lacks understanding of these things."

Falcon took a deep breath, seeing clearly what he had brought on Taylor. "How do I help her?"

"You can't." His grandfather shook his head. "If you go to her, try to rescue her now when they are expecting you, she could be killed."

Chapter Thirteen

Taylor realized in less than twenty-four hours that Falcon wasn't coming. And she knew why.

Wolf and his minions waited, watching. Taylor could feel their tension, and sometimes their fear. She busied herself with reading, writing, trying to remember what her mother had taught her about knitting. Sometimes she took long walks, always accompanied by Wolf's sentinels, Ziha and Rose. She was allowed to call her mother once, and let her know that she was fine. Occasionally she could send her a letter that they supposedly mailed. When she needed something, Wolf's apparent right hand, Rhine, brought it back for her.

They weren't nice to her, but they weren't unkind, either. They seemed to expect her to try to make an escape, and Taylor took pleasure in keeping them guessing by being a sunny version of the houseguest that never left.

The midwife came every month, and though her eyes seemed sympathetic, Taylor did not trust her. So she said nothing to her beyond answering the basic medical questions she asked.

One thing she knew for certain: this time of her life

would not last forever. What she and Falcon shared would.

Wolf wouldn't break their spirits.

In fact, Taylor knew one other thing: with each day Emma grew inside her, her love for Falcon grew deeper.

FALCON THOUGHT HE WOULD always remember Christmas Day as the worst day of his life, the day his past and his future had collided. He desperately wanted to find Taylor, take care of her and protect her the way he'd always promised he would.

He'd never felt this dark envelopment of fear.

But then January went by, February followed fast, March slipped into spring. Falcon knew Taylor had to feel betrayed. She would have believed he would come for her.

But he didn't.

"Nothing?" Galen asked, coming in from the barn, where Falcon sat staring toward the canyons.

"Nothing. No signal. It's like Wolf was never here."

Galen shook his head. "Maybe Running Bear is wrong. Maybe you should find her. I'm sure her mother is terribly upset and thinks you've abandoned her daughter."

"Her mother says Taylor's fine. Taylor called her once and said so. Every now and again she gets a letter, postmarked Colorado. Running Bear says Taylor is not in Colorado." He sighed. "Running Bear says it's a diversion."

"Why would they bother with diversionary tactics when they left plenty of tracks?"

"The chief believes it's to confuse any law enforcement who might be looking for Taylor. They're keeping her mother calm."

"But hoping you'll show up so they can trap you?"

"I guess. Although I don't have any more knowledge than anyone else around here." Falcon resented the fact that his uncle seemed to take special glee in singling him out for attention.

"You're the one expecting a child. You'd be most likely to crack."

"Crack Wolf's head wide open."

"I'll go in your place," Galen said. "We won't mention it to Grandfather."

"As if he wouldn't figure it out. Thanks, Galen, but I can't ask that of you."

Galen clapped him on the back. "Better to ride out to Colorado than sit here doing nothing. We could use a road trip."

Falcon perked up. "I'd give anything to find Taylor."

"Let's go," Galen prompted. "Action is always better than inaction, right?"

Falcon tried to think logically over the sudden thundering of his heart. "Then again, we don't want to go on a wild-goose chase. Maybe it would be best to press Running Bear for information. You know he knows more than he's telling."

Galen nodded. "I'll pack the truck. You get what you can out of Running Bear. Good luck with that."

"GRANDFATHER," Ash said, coming upon him near the stone circle, where she'd hoped to find him. "Let me go find Taylor. Falcon's about to explode. It's killing him."

Running Bear grunted. "You can't always save your brothers, little one."

"I could rescue Taylor," Ash said.

He shook his head. "This is Falcon's battle. It is his test. You have to let him win it on his own. It's not good to interfere with another person's destiny."

"I don't believe in destiny," Ash said.

"I know," he said wryly. "You've told me a hundred times."

She leaned her head against the old man's shoulder. "Teach me the ways, Grandfather."

"Why? Why should I teach the sacred ways to one who doesn't believe? I don't even know that you honor the sprits anymore," he said gruffly.

"You should teach me," Ash said, sitting down next to him, her ankles crossed, "because you are old. You won't live forever, as much as I would prefer that you did."

He grunted again. "You should show respect to your elders. You didn't live with the tribe long enough to know this. It shows."

She laughed. "If I respected my elders, I'd let my brothers have the upper hand. And I think we'd all admit that we prefer me keeping them on their toes. But I respect *you*," she said, leaning her head against his shoulder once more.

He was silent for a moment. "When did you figure out that you were the favored one of my heart?"

"When you told my mother you felt certain she should have one more child. You were waiting for me."

"Yes, and when I got you, I wanted to put you back. You were an untamable spirit."

"Just like my grandfather," she said fondly. "And you did not want to put me back. You used to take me on special pony rides. You told me stories of the spirits at night, talked to me about the stars that guided me."

"I did the same for your brothers."

"But they didn't get to wear the chief's headdress," Ash reminded him. "I did, and I knew I was special."

"You were like a cloud, going here and there and anywhere. Floating on any breeze."

"Grandfather, did you know that clouds are basically water droplets and ice?"

"Yes, little cloud," her grandfather said, giving up. "Why do you want to learn the ways?"

"Because it's time," she said simply. "So you can rest."

"I am not ready to rest."

"It's okay, Grandfather," Ash said softly. "It will take you years to teach me everything."

He was silent a long time, maybe an hour. Ash sat still next to him, knowing not to speak. Finally, Running Bear said, "Walk two miles, where you will find an empty cave. Sit there."

"For how long?"

He didn't look at her. "Until you know the spirits."

"What about Falcon and Taylor? Why can't I just go shoot Uncle Wolf?" Ash asked impatiently. "If he's the ringleader and the only connection to us, I think one single sniper shot would take care of the problem."

Running Bear looked at her. "If killing my son would solve the problem, I would do it myself."

She hung her head. "It can't be easy knowing that your son has a dark heart." She looked up again. "I just want to help Taylor so much. She helped me."

"What did you not learn?"

She sighed. "That I have to let Taylor and Falcon fight their own battle. Their destiny is for them alone."

"Go, cloud."

FALCON FOUND RUNNING BEAR in the most unlikely place: sitting in Fiona's kitchen, eating cookies and drinking coffee, as if nothing in the world was wrong.

"Just the man I need to see," Falcon said.

"The man you need to see!" Fiona exclaimed. "What am I, chopped liver?"

His grandfather's eyes wrinkled up with what could be taken as a pleasant expression. "Respect your aunt."

"I do. She's the one sane thing around here." He hugged Fiona. "Burke's pretty sane, too, though, thank heaven."

Fiona smiled. "Sit. Let me pour you a mug."

"I need to talk to Grandfather."

His grandfather's eyes met his. "Talking is easier on a full stomach," Fiona said. "I've got a pot roast on and blackberry pie for desert."

Food sounded good, but information better. "Walk with me," Falcon told his grandfather.

"I just got him sitting," Fiona said. "Sit with him and make him eat, and I'll leave the room." She pulled off her apron. "I can tell this is an aunt-free conversation."

"Thanks, Aunt Fiona." Falcon accepted the cookies and coffee his aunt gave him, and when Fiona had sailed from the kitchen, blowing a kiss behind her, he sat next to his grandfather. "I can't find Ash anywhere."

"Ashlyn is studying the old ways."

Falcon nodded. "She mentioned she was going to talk to you. We're thin here, and I'm leaving. Galen has offered to ride shotgun."

"Going to find something?"

He nodded. "It's time for Taylor to come back home. My daughter will be born soon. I want her born in Diablo."

"Have you found what you were missing?"

Falcon gazed at his grandfather. In the bright, sunny kitchen, Running Bear looked like a painted wood carving come to life. Falcon always thought the chief looked solid, indestructible, timeless. "I'm missing my woman and my child. That's all I need."

Running Bear nodded. "That is right. It's good to know your soul."

"More than that. She's my spirit."

"You asked Taylor to stay with you forever?"

"She asked me to marry her, I'm pretty sure, on Christmas Eve. Just before she was taken." His whole body turned cold at the memory. "I would have said yes if I'd had more time. Someone told me to let her make the decision, to wait for her. So then I did, but then she was gone." His body grew chilled at the memory. "I can't forget it. One minute we were happy and the next minute my world exploded."

"That makes you angry."

"Yes. And scared." He *had* been scared. It had been hard to accept that he couldn't protect the woman he loved and the child he hoped to meet one day.

"And now?"

Falcon swallowed. "I'll always hate Wolf. But I know that he wants me, and I'm going to give myself up. Make him send Taylor here. Then he can try to get whatever information he's looking for out of me."

"Does the mouse walk into the snake's jaws?"

Falcon blinked. "Not the mouse. The mongoose has no fear."

"Because the mongoose can strike first if it chooses. The snake fears it. And fear is the key."

His eyes went wide. "You think I should attack Wolf?"

The chief shrugged. "Nature teaches good lessons."

Attack Wolf. How? In what way?

"Are you not the thinker?" the chief asked softly. "Your siblings say you are the smart one, the one whose mind knows no boundaries of imagination."

Falcon got up and went to look out the window. Galen was packing the truck, but in the distance Falcon saw a shadow, a flying mane, a tossing head dark on the horizon. His heart raced into overdrive.

"I am the hunted one, aren't I?" he said, turning to his grandfather.

His worst nightmare.

"Only you can walk the path. No one can tell you your own truth," Running Bear said. He looked at him for a long time, then said, "Glenn, Montana, is where you'll find what you are looking for."

"Taylor's letters to her mother are postmarked Colorado."

Running Bear nodded. "Nothing is ever exactly what it seems."

Chapter Fourteen

The babble of low voices in the next room caught Taylor's attention. She moved to the wall to listen.

"It's the end of April," Ziha said. "He's not coming."

"Falcon Callahan isn't coming," Rose said, "so you misjudged their relationship, Wolf."

"She's having a baby," Wolf said.

"Do we know it's Falcon's?" Ziha asked. "Just because she got pregnant doesn't mean it's his baby. He would have been here by now if he cared. So this mission has no purpose. And I'm out of here."

Taylor put her ear tight against the wall so she could hear the argument better. Everyone sounded very frustrated, which made her smile to herself.

"You can't leave," Wolf said.

"Yes, we can. We didn't sign up for you picking on an innocent woman. If you read her letters to her mother you'd know that she never mentions Falcon. Or any of the Callahans. She's going to have that baby any day now, and I definitely want no part of holding a woman who should be with her mother when her child is born," Ziha said.

"We quit," Rose said. "Taylor's a nice person, and

you just can't handle the fact that you made a mistake. This isn't the way to flush Falcon out."

"If you want to get the information on your brothers so badly, why don't you just hold the old lady for ransom? The Callahans would sing like birds to get Fiona back," a male voice said.

Rhine. He was a general troublemaker, in Taylor's estimation. He didn't look like part of the tribe, but he seemed more like a hired gun, and of all of them, she steered clear of Rhine the most. Especially since he probably still held a grudge about her shooting him.

"I think about taking Fiona," Wolf said. "I'm just not sure how much she knows. I think the brothers are the only ones who know anything."

"Okay, well, your plan of kidnapping women to get the men to squeal needs to be abandoned," Ziha said. "You'll have to figure it out on your own. We're leaving on the next bus."

Just then Taylor heard a "psst!" and she glanced at the window.

Falcon.

She gasped and flew to the window, opening it. "What are you doing here? They're in the other room. You have to leave!"

"I am leaving. We're leaving. Get your stuff." He looked at her. "You're more beautiful than the last time I saw you, by the way."

Taylor smiled, but her heart raced as she grabbed her few things and crammed them into a large purse. Falcon helped her out the window, and they hurried to the truck.

Taylor climbed in next to Galen, who was driving.

Falcon jumped in next to her, sandwiching her, and Galen put the truck in Reverse.

"Hang on just a minute," Falcon said. "I want to leave a parting gift."

"Do we have to do parting gifts?" Taylor asked, worried. "They're arguing fiercely in there. We could be thirty minutes down the road before they figure out I'm gone."

"Life's no fun without party prizes." Galen halted the truck. "Go for it."

"Oh, great. I'm riding with Cassidy and Sundance," Taylor said.

"Nope," Falcon said, squeezing off a shot that instantly flattened Wolf's rear tire. "You're riding with the Callahans." He took out a second tire, and Galen sped off. "Lucky for you."

"I knew you'd come."

Falcon didn't know what to think about that. Taylor didn't seem annoyed or upset at all, and if he'd been in her place, he certainly would have been. "I would have been here sooner, but—"

"Running Bear said you would come when the ice and snow melted, and tempers grew hot. That's exactly what's happening back there. Tempers are flaring."

Galen laughed. Falcon shook his head. "When did you talk to the chief?"

Taylor smiled at him, and it warmed every corner of his heart. "He came every month to check on me, usually around the first, a few days after the midwife."

Falcon's gaze fell to her stomach. "Is my baby all right?"

"Our baby is fine," she reassured him.

He took a deep breath, feeling immensely better now

that he had Taylor back. "Back to Running Bear—how could he see you every month?"

She shrugged. "He showed up at the same window you did. No one ever saw him. The sentries were posted, and I was never alone in the house, but somehow he still managed. I like your grandfather," Taylor said, her eyes sparkling.

"He's a wily old man," Falcon muttered. "Crazy like a fox."

He leaned over and kissed her, no longer able to hold back from touching her, holding her. "We have unfinished business, dating back to Christmas Eve."

"That's a night I'll always remember," Taylor said.

"What happened? One minute you were behind me, and then you were gone." Fury filled him all over again, remembering how Taylor had been taken.

"I guess Ziha and Rose were hiding in the entryway. Someone knocked at the kitchen door to divert you, and they spirited me away out the front. They must have given me something that knocked me out, because I don't remember very much until I woke up in Montana." Taylor shook her head. "It's kind of funny, though. Back there they were just giving your uncle their notice. They said you were never coming, and they were sick of his plan of action."

Falcon smiled grimly. "I was coming. Grandfather was worried about what would happen to you if I showed up too soon. He felt like time needed to pass for them to get lax."

"That's what happened. Your grandfather told me to stay at peace, lie low, make myself happy, and that soon they would begin to get nervous, second-guess themselves. And grow slack. That's exactly what happened." She smiled at Falcon. "Rose and Ziha weren't bad, actually, once we got to know each other. Rose is pretty sweet and seems like she doesn't really belong with Wolf's gang. I don't think she and Wolf like each other very much. When I needed new maternity clothes, Rose and Ziha went into town and bought me some things. And I was teaching them card games and cooking skills."

He shook his head. "Generous of you. I probably would have considered judicious poisoning if I'd been in your place."

"Not generous." She leaned against him. "I just trusted that everything would work out. By the way, your uncle is really frustrated. He's going to be superhot that you got me out from right underneath his nose."

"That's just fine," Falcon said. "Galen, don't slow down until we hit the county line. Because if Wolf catches up to us, I'm pretty sure I'll put a bullet right where it will do the most good."

"You know Running Bear said absolutely not on the easy solution," Galen said.

"I know." Falcon wanted to do nothing more than take out his uncle and end the turmoil. Wouldn't everything be solved then? They could all go on living their normal lives. Their Callahan cousins could come home. He and his siblings could go back—

They could never go back. Rancho Diablo had become their home. The Callahans were their family. And they knew each other better now than they had since before their parents had gone away. He remembered those days. They'd been the best times of their lives, long childhood days among their tribe, with each other.

Taylor put her hand in his. "It's going to be all right."

He nodded. "I know."

Now that he had her back, that was exactly how he felt.

"Well, kids, this is where I get off this train," Galen said. "You're on your own from here."

ONCE TAYLOR WAS ALONE with Falcon, she suddenly felt shy. They'd lost a precious four months and she felt far from her dream of them getting to know each other slowly before Emma was born.

He drove from the airport in Helena, and Taylor thought it was probably good that they were in a truck together for the next two days.

"I'd like to pick up where we left off," Falcon said, "but I don't know how possible that is."

She thought about Christmas Eve, and how for one shining moment, she'd felt hopeful for a future together. "I don't know, either."

He moved his hat back a little, a gesture that she'd learned to recognize meant he was deep in thought. "Maybe we just go easy. Figure things out slowly."

She nodded. "Sometimes slow is better."

"Although I've had enough of slow. It's frustrating, because I'm pretty sure I remember you proposing to me. Or saying yes. It doesn't matter. Either way, I'm certain that you'd just agreed to hit up an altar with me, before you were kidnapped. I'm sorry as hell about that. The guilt is just tearing me up."

"It's not your fault," Taylor quickly said. "And anyway, I knew what I was getting into when I... When we—"

"That's the thing. I don't think you could have known. I know what Jillian told you, and I know you took her advice to heart. The whole December dead-line thing was a chance for you to find something bet-ter, have time to realize that a Callahan was the last thing you wanted."

"I make up my own mind," Taylor said impatiently. "I knew the risks, and I didn't care."

"I care," Falcon said. "I don't want this for my wife and child."

"So what?" Taylor demanded. "So you're just going to give up, walk away? Send me off to Hell's Colony with the rest of your family?"

He perked up. "That's an idea with some merit."

"No, it's not. I've been gone for four months! I'm not going anywhere else." She frowned. "I'll have you know I've lived in the belly of the beast for months with your uncle Wolf. And I'm fine. It wasn't what I wanted to do with my life, but I learned patience. I learned what mat-ters most to me in life. How is that different from Ash or you going off for days at a time to figure out your life? Commune with nature or whatever you call it?"

He smiled at her. "Listening to the spirits of our an-cestors may be what you're thinking of."

She shook her head. "I'll decide what bothers me, thanks. If you can't handle your life, that's your issue. Not mine. Wolf barely talked to me. There were days I wasn't sure why he'd picked me. Ash or Fiona would be far more likely to raise a hue and cry from the Cal-lahans—and they have answers about your family that I don't know. Frankly, it was just a nice vacation in Mon-tana for me, a beautiful state, a perfect place for Emma and me to hibernate."

His gaze slipped over to her very large belly. "When does Emma come out of hibernation?"

"I haven't had a prenatal checkup since December, but at the time, the doctor put my due date at about a month from now." She couldn't wait. Every day brought her closer. And now that Falcon had come for her, she had the comfort of knowing that her baby—their baby— would be born in Diablo. It was perfect.

"Wow," Falcon said, and she realized he'd turned a bit pale.

"What?"

"A month to go? And you haven't seen a doctor?"

"I wasn't totally without care. It just wasn't the sort of care I would have gotten with my own obstetrician. But I feel great. In fact, I've never felt better. It might have been all the good clean Montana air."

"I should have put you on the plane instead of Galen," Falcon grumbled. "I should have called Rafe and had him pick you up in the family jet. You shouldn't be rid- ing in a truck for two days."

"I'm fine. I'll let you know when I'm not." She stared out at the beautiful landscape rushing past her window. "If you're going to be a worrywart for the next two days, I will fly back."

"I'm not trying to be a worrywart, I'm trying to take care of you."

"I don't need to be taken care of, Falcon. I want you to ignore the last four months and think of me as your partner."

He rubbed his chin. "I don't know if I can do that. Do you understand that other men don't have to worry about their women being kidnapped because of a fam- ily feud? That's what I face every day. It's a damn help- less feeling."

She understood, but at the same time, living in the

past would mean Wolf won. She couldn't let him win, for Emma's sake. After a long moment, Taylor knew she had to be completely honest. She put a hand against his forearm. "We have to focus on what we're doing, not what Wolf did, or this isn't going to work, Falcon. And your uncle wins. Because nothing would make him happier than to know he'd destroyed a Callahan's happiness."

Chapter Fifteen

Falcon pulled into Rancho Diablo, his mind racing with how he was going to protect his new family now that they'd returned. Taylor had a point: Wolf wouldn't bother her again, because Falcon hadn't gone after her. Everything had played out just as Running Bear had said.

But a baby…would that be a whole different scenario? Falcon doubted Running Bear could stop him, much less Taylor, if Emma became a hostage.

"Quit worrying," Taylor said, easing herself out of the truck as he cut the engine. "I can hear you worrying from two feet away. Nothing's going to happen, Falcon."

How could he be sure? Ash wasn't here right now—she was still on some kind of spiritual bender. Tighe and Dante weren't here; they were enjoying the heck out of the rodeo circuit, apparently. Falcon figured those two would never return to Rancho Diablo. Jace was around somewhere, and Galen had probably gotten back by now. Sloan and Kendall had gone to join the other family members at Dark Diablo, wanting the twins to have other cousins to play with. At the moment, they were filling in with hired help at Rancho Diablo, and that presented problems of its own.

"I'm not worrying. I'm just thinking."

Taylor shook her head and went in the kitchen door, breathing a sigh of relief when she entered Fiona's sanctuary. "Oh, my. I missed this. I miss my mother, too." She looked at Falcon. "I may stay at my house, even though Mom isn't there right now. You'll fret less."

He looked at her pumpkin-shaped tummy. She was beautiful—stunning and cute and everything he'd ever wanted in a woman. How had that happened? He'd watched her for many long months, trying to figure out how he could get a girl like her to go out with a guy—a renegade—like him. And then one day he'd blurted out his true feelings, that he wanted to marry her.

He loved her so much it was like his heart was a crazy, wild thing that settled only when she was around. "You might have missed home, but I missed you."

She slipped her arms around his neck. "It was harder on you than it was on me."

"I don't know. I'm pretty sure I couldn't be stuck in a cabin with Uncle Wolf for months." He didn't even like to think about it. But she was in his arms, and this was new, and yet familiar, and he loved her more than he could have ever imagined loving a woman.

She stood on her toes, pressed a kiss against his lips. He closed his eyes, enjoying the tenderness she gave him, then kissed her back with all the wistfulness he'd felt, and the ache of missing her. If a simple gesture could speak the words of his heart, he wanted his kiss to tell Taylor how sorry he was, how much he respected her, how much he needed her.

She sank back on her feet, and he reluctantly released her. Missed her already. "Thank you," he said.

"For what?"

"For forgiving me. For not hating me. I was so afraid you would."

"That's because you don't believe here." She put her hand over his heart. "You're going to have to start believing that what Wolf does, however bad, is going to come out good for us in the end. I believe it."

After a moment, Falcon nodded. Her gaze was so clear, so honest and sincere, that he knew Taylor had made a decision to believe in him, believe in their relationship. He could do no less. "Okay. I'm going to work on it. I can be more appreciative of what's going right for us."

"Good." She smiled, her face luminous. "I'm glad. We have a lot to look forward to."

He felt hope lift him. "I agree."

"Good." She took his hand. "Because my water just broke, and I'm very certain Emma wants her father to be the happiest man in Diablo tonight."

"I'M NOT GOING TO SAY I didn't panic," Falcon said proudly staring in at his new daughter in the bassinet in the hospital nursery. "I know I panicked. Taylor was calm, not rattled at all. She took a shower—she insisted she had to have a real shower after riding in a truck for two days—and then I drove her to her house, she packed some things, and I brought her here. My heart was racing faster than a car engine, and when they wheeled her back to the O.R., I thought for a minute I was going to black out." He looked at Fiona and his sister. "Knowing that the woman who is having your child is undergoing a C-section is worse than being in the military. I saw a lot of stuff overseas, but I was never as torn up as I was when they took Taylor back." He gazed at Emma, who was sleeping peacefully in her bassinet. His heart swelled with joy.

"Well, I'm proud of you, brother." Ash patted his shoulder. "Emma is beautiful. Of course, she looks like her mother, thankfully. And I love her sweet blue aura. Such a happy baby."

Fiona let out a sigh of happiness. "I'm so glad Taylor was here when Emma was born. I don't think I could have borne it if she'd had the baby in Montana with Wolf and those dreadful minions of his." She shuddered. "Dreadful, the whole thing. Wolf has got to be stopped, and soon. Or I'm going to do it myself. I'd have no problem serving him a big helping of apricot preserves with a splash of arsenic."

"Aunt Fiona." Falcon grinned.

"It's all right," Ash said. "I like having a bloodthirsty aunt. It's kind of cool."

"Don't encourage her." Falcon stared at Emma, seeing her tiny fingernails and shell-shaped eyelids. She was so adorable that his heart filled up despite the cracks it had suffered in the past few months.

Taylor had given him an amazing gift.

"I don't need any encouragement," Fiona said. "I think Emma would expect her great-aunt to be the standard bearer for the females of the family."

"No!" both Falcon and Ash exclaimed.

"The chief says we're not to hurt Uncle Wolf," Falcon said, and Fiona said, "Humph. He said you Callahans can't. I'm a good Irish girl whose family saw The Trouble. I have no problem with spicing up some jelly for your benighted uncle."

She went blithely off, heading toward Taylor's room.

Falcon looked at his daughter. "You don't think Fiona would do anything rash, do you?"

"Sure. She's Fiona," Ash said. "She's a fighter. Don't doubt it."

He didn't. "Discourage her any way you can."

"Okay, that will work. She'll listen to us, because she listens to anybody." Ash's tone was sarcastic. She leaned closer to the nursery glass, considering the newborn. "Maybe Emma inherited your brains. One thing I can say about you, you got more than your fair share of gray matter, dear brother." Ash gasped. "Maybe she got my heart!"

He grinned. "Well, as family gifts go, that would be a good one." His sister had a heart like a lion. Between Taylor, Fiona, Ash, her grandmother Julia, Emma had all the genes for—

"She's going to be a warrior," Ash said in a wondering tone, and a tickle of premonition slid over Falcon.

"No. She's not. This all stops now," he said determinedly. "I'm going to keep her in a school for young ladies—"

"Which are great places for a girl to learn how to hold her own," Ash said.

"And you are not to teach her to shoot, or hunt, or… any of the ways."

Ash looked up at him. "What is the matter with you? Why wouldn't you want your daughter to learn our ways?"

"Because," Falcon said simply. He couldn't explain his fear; he just was afraid. Because if he was the hunted one Running Bear had spoken of, then his daughter might be, too.

"You can't keep her in a bottle, brother," Ash said.

"If she's meant to be a lion, she'll be a lion. You can't make her a sparrow if that's not her path."

"You don't believe in destiny. Or paths."

Ash looked back at Emma. "Maybe I've changed my mind."

Falcon stepped away from the window. "I intend to protect my family from now on. I'm never again going through what I went through, and my family is never being taken from me."

Ash gazed at him. She looked as if she was about to say something, but Falcon turned and walked away.

A MONTH LATER, after Taylor and Falcon had been through several shifts of night feedings, learning to diaper on the fly, and laughing at cute baby faces, Taylor began to realize that her husband had changed.

She looked out the window at Falcon. He had Emma strapped in a harness, cradling her little head with a big hand. "He never puts her down," she told her mother, who'd come to see the baby.

"It's good to see a father adore his child," Mary said. "Your father was like that with you. He would have loved little Emma."

"I know." Taylor watched Falcon direct workers to different areas of the corral, putting several horses out for the day. "I barely get to hold her."

"Don't complain," Mary said. "Falcon wants you to rest. Most mothers would love a husband that shares the duties."

Taylor shook her head. "He doesn't even put her down very often when he's inside."

Her mom looked at her. "Well, he's a new dad. I'm sure that's all it is."

But Taylor didn't think it was that simple. "Ever since he brought me back from Montana, Falcon's been more of a bodyguard to Emma than a new dad learning the ropes."

"Can you blame him?" Mary asked softly. "Falcon went through hell while you were gone. He blames himself. He's not going to let anything happen to his daughter."

"How long does it last?"

"What? New dad syndrome?" Mary shrugged. "Probably after he's run off the first twenty guys who propose to Emma, and he's finally settled on the one he can stomach taking his daughter away from him."

Fiona sailed into the room, her usual cheery disposition on full display. "Isn't this a lovely June day? I just love June." She looked at Mary, her gaze conspiratorial. "I always think of weddings when the calendar page is on June, don't you, Mary?"

Mary nodded. "June is such a lovely, traditional month for weddings."

They looked at Taylor. She shook her head. "We haven't discussed it."

"Not even once?" Fiona asked, her voice disappointed.

"Not even once." Everything had happened too quickly.

"What are you waiting on?" Fiona demanded, then sighed. "I'm sorry, it's none of my business. I'm nosy, I've always been nosy. It's my worst fault."

"As faults go, it's not that terrible," Taylor said, trying to be diplomatic.

Fiona looked out at Emma and Falcon. "It's just that my friends at the Books'n'Bingo Society have been asking, of course, since it is June, if they should mark any certain date on their very busy calendars. So many weddings in Diablo, and of course, no one wants to miss a single one."

"Really?" Mary said. "Who else is getting married?"

Fiona blinked. "Well, a few people. But no matter. There doesn't need to be a wedding. We had a christening, after all, and at least that's something."

Mary nodded. "It's something."

They both looked at Taylor, their gazes imploring.

She sighed. "Falcon needs time to adjust to fatherhood."

Fiona glanced out the window. "He looks adjusted to me."

"Marriage is a tricky thing," Mary murmured. "We'll just tell the ladies and Jillian that a baby shower is all we can accept at this time."

"Did someone offer a baby shower?" Taylor asked.

"And a wedding shower," Fiona said with the most pitiful expression Taylor had ever seen. "Our friends are a bit party-hard-y." She looked mournful. "There was some suggestion that maybe the two of you need your own place—not that I agree, of course—and as such, perhaps a house warming party needed to be penciled on the calendar, as well. June was shaping up to be a busy month," Fiona finished, looked sadder with each word.

"We don't need a…" Taylor stopped speaking, glancing back and forth between her mother and Fiona. "I mean, how very kind of everyone to want to help us." She took a deep breath, dived into the deep end of her fears. "Maybe I could mention these kind offers to Falcon—" the ladies' faces brightened considerably "—and see how he feels. But I'm not making any promises," she said hurriedly. "And as a matter of fact, if he even looks a little intimidated, I'm not saying another word about it to him. Ever."

The ladies nodded. "I can accept that," Fiona said.

"Me, too," Mary said. "Just a tiny mention ought to be enough to get him to run with it. Men actually like marriage more than they admit."

Taylor wasn't so certain. Once upon a time, Falcon had been very gung ho about marriage.

She hadn't quite known what to make of it. Had no desire to bring it up.

But it wasn't about the parties or the showers, and she knew it, even though her mother and Fiona had couched it that way. It was about Emma, and building a family that couldn't be broken.

Yet one thing had changed since the night Falcon had first proposed to her. That rowdy cowboy who'd surprised her with his proposal nearly a year ago in Jillian's diner had said that after they got married and had a baby, they could figure out if they could still stand each other. And if they did, maybe they could sit on the porch together. He'd told her, in that teasing way he had, that he hadn't wanted to work hard for a wife. And then he'd very subtly promised to make love to her every which way from Sunday.

He'd barely kissed her since she'd been back from Montana.

Not once.

"THIS IS WHAT IS KNOWN as an intervention, brother," Ash said, and the meeting commenced in the upstairs library. Galen, Ash, Sloan, Falcon and Jace were in attendance—and of course, little Emma.

Falcon looked at his daughter as she sat cradled in his arms. "Your first meeting," he told her, "and they hold an intervention. What a silly thing to say in a little girl's presence." He glared at his sister. "Are you talking to me when you say intervention?"

Ash nodded. "Yes, I am. We all are."

"Interventions may be necessary around this joint," Falcon said, "but not for me. I'm doing better than I ever have."

They all stared back at him, like a nestful of baby barn owls. "What?"

"Let Aunt Ash hold Emma," Ash said, sidling over to take her tiny niece.

He leaned back to elude his sister's greedy fingers. "She's napping. Never wake a sleeping baby is the rule of thumb I salute."

"She's not asleep," Jace said. "It looks to me as if Emma's wondering why her father is telling a fib. Give her to Uncle Jace. She prefers me, I can tell."

"No, thanks. She just got comfortable." What was with his family trying to take his child? It was annoying.

"So, how's Taylor?" Galen asked.

"Fine." Falcon smiled down at his baby, delighted when she grinned back at him. "Oh, there's a smile. And it's not gas, either. That was an old wives' tale created to scare fathers away from their children."

Sloan sighed. "Falcon, I have two babies. Twins. And I don't hold the two of them combined as much as you hold Emma. Although I hold them a lot and hug them and read to them nightly. You're going to have permanent hooks in your elbows if you don't take a break from holding her. Give her to me. Uncle Sloan has plenty of experience."

"What is it with you guys?" Falcon demanded. "Emma is fine right where she is. She likes to be with me. I calm her down. And besides, I like holding my daughter."

"Yes, we see," Ash said, "but if you held your wife half as much, you might be a husband as well as a father."

He gawked at his siblings. "Is that what this is all about? Taylor?"

"We have noticed that you seem a bit more enamored of your baby than your lady," Galen said, "and no doubt you don't mean to put that impression across. So for tonight's meeting, we'd like to offer to watch Emma, up here in this nice, comfortable room, where we'll all attend her every smile and waved finger," he cajoled. "Perhaps you'd like to take Taylor out on a date."

"A couple's night out," Ash said, "to give you both a break from hanging around all of us."

"Well," Falcon said, looking down at Emma. "I guess we could go out for a little while. Taylor hasn't had a night out since she's been back." He frowned, thinking. "Yeah, maybe a night at a nice restaurant would be good for her." He got up, walked to the door.

"Wait a minute," Ash said, walking after him. "Aren't you forgetting something? Like us, your amazing quartet of babysitters?" She reached to take Emma, and Falcon moved his arms so his sister couldn't touch the baby.

"We'll just take her with us. Thank you," Falcon said politely, and they all groaned.

"That's it," Galen said. "Sit down, Falcon."

"Okay," he said reluctantly, not certain what "it" was, exactly. Now that they'd mentioned taking Taylor on a date, he was ready to go. "Hurry, though, because I want to give Taylor plenty of time to get ready."

"Jace, pour our brother a small one," Galen said. "Ash, begin."

Jace handed Falcon a whiskey, which he accepted with some hesitation. His sibs were clearly up to no good—and it had to do with Emma. He had news for them: he had supersonic radar when it came to his daughter. They had a bond where they practically read each other's mind. Of course, Emma didn't do much reading—she was so very young—but he knew what she was thinking practically every second.

"Brother," Ash said, "you've got to give the baby up."

"Never," Falcon said, stunned, and Jace sighed heavily.

"Give the baby to other people to take care of," Jace clarified. "I don't know if you've even showered in the past month, because you hold her constantly."

"I've showered," Falcon said defensively. "We shower together, and then I hand her to Taylor. Well, I hold Emma under the spray, and she seems happy, and then Taylor takes her off for a little rubadub in some lavender bath stuff. Then I get dressed, brush my teeth, and take Emma down the hall for our nightly reading. Usually the *Wall Street Journal,* but sometimes we deviate and read *The Wild Baby Goes to Sea,* but sometimes Emma wants something more—"

"I can't take it," Ash said. "Falcon, you've changed so much from the man who was determined to win Taylor that I don't even recognize you. You've become a mother hen. And that is not a compliment. Now give me the baby and go take your wife out somewhere! Anywhere!"

He gulped. "You guys are being so weird," he said, but he began to see a sliver of daylight. His siblings thought he was a mother hen—when once he'd been known as a hard-bitten military operative. "The thing is, I know that if Emma's with me, she's safe—"

"We know," Galen said. "Hand us Emma."

They all moved close, and he reluctantly gave Emma into his siblings' eager hands. "I hadn't realized I was spending so much time with Emma." He looked at his family's sympathetic faces. "Did Taylor mention it to you?"

"No." Ash shook her head. "Taylor never says a word that's not pleasant. That's why she's the best. And you're the best. We want you to find each other again."

"We—" He stopped. Considered what his family understood that he had not. "Thanks, guys."

He kissed Emma tenderly on her head, saw her clear eyes looking back at him from Ash's arms. She was fine. He could see that.

But he needed to take care of her future now.

He headed out the door.

Chapter Sixteen

Taylor looked up as Falcon hurried into the kitchen at Rancho Diablo, where she was making lasagna for dinner. Fiona had disappeared, so Taylor had taken it upon herself to begin placing the layers of ingredients in the long pan. "Where's Emma?"

He stopped and looked at her. "Uh, my family has her."

"Oh. Okay." She went back to carefully building the lasagna.

"Taylor," Falcon said, "do you want to go out to dinner tonight?"

She looked up. "I'm almost finished making dinner."

He scratched his head. "Yeah, I see that."

She smiled. "Another time, maybe."

He hesitated, looked at her. Taylor watched him curiously. "Is something wrong?"

"Not wrong. I'm just trying to ask you out on a date, and obviously not doing a very good job of it."

"Ohh," Taylor said. "Have you been talking to Fiona and my mother?"

He blinked. "No, but I have been read the riot act by my family. They seem to think I pay too much attention to Emma and not enough to you. I agree with them."

Taylor stopped layering. "I just thought you had new-dad symptoms."

He drummed his fingers on the kitchen counter. "Let's do something spontaneous."

She washed her hands and covered the lasagna pan. "Our first and only date was ghost hunting. We never found any, though. I was always a little disappointed about that. We did find your uncle Wolf, however, and I guess he qualifies as a specter of some kind."

"Yeah." Falcon pondered that for a minute. "That was fine for a girl I was just dating. We've got a daughter now. I need to step up my game."

"That sounds…interesting. I'll go dress appropriately."

He followed her upstairs. They slept in separate rooms since she was still staying at Rancho Diablo; Emma slept in a crib in the upstairs nursery. Taylor suspected Falcon mostly slept in there to be near his daughter—she'd found him a few times asleep in the rocking chair when she went in to check on Emma.

"I need to change, too. I'll meet you in the kitchen in thirty?"

Her gaze swept him. "Don't change too much, Falcon. I like you just the way you used to come into the diner," Taylor said. "Handsome. Sexy."

He perked up. "You think I'm sexy?"

"Maybe a little. Don't let it swell your head."

TWO AND A HALF HOURS later they were sitting at a rodeo in Santa Fe. Taylor looked darling in blue jeans—she claimed she was halfway back to her old size, grumbling about it a bit, but he thought she looked more beautiful than ever—and a white blouse. Her chocolate hair was tied back with a white pearl clip. It had been so long since it had just been the two of them together, having fun and relaxing.

"Good thing my family saved me from myself," Falcon said. "I've been missing all the really good stuff."

She smiled, and he felt as if he practically fell into her eyes. "I got a little redirection from my family, too," she admitted.

Once they'd gotten in the truck, he'd felt he could drive for hours with Taylor. No Wolf to worry about, no drama, just the two of them, the way he'd wanted it to be last fall. "I should never have accepted Jillian's challenge. I should have just dated you. Heck, I should have stood under your window and yodeled every night for you."

Her eyes crinkled. "Yodeled?"

"It's the best I can do. But I can yodel fairly decently." He leaned back against the bleacher in back of him. "Tonight we're watching the young guys try their hand at the rodeo. Dante and Tighe did this for a while when they were juniors. They weren't too bad."

She watched the young children rush out for the mutton busting. Boys and girls scrambled to get in line for their chance on a well-built sheep. None of them stayed on very long, and it was cute to see them try. "I wonder if Emma will want to do that."

"No way. I won't let her."

Taylor looked at him. "Why?"

"I don't want her to be a rodeo girl. She's going to go to a finishing school somewhere, and I never want to see her in a pair of cowboy boots."

Taylor blinked. "I don't believe what I'm hearing."

He shrugged. "I'd bottle her and put her away until she was thirty, if I could."

"Falcon, you can't protect her forever." Taylor gazed at him with a soft smile. "You're still scared, aren't you?"

"Me? Scared?" He shook his head. "I'm a retired sniper. I'm not scared of much, doll."

That won him a frown. "Then you can't say Emma can't ever mutton bust. And that she has to go to a finishing school."

"Education is important to our family. We all worked hard so Galen could finish medical school. We tried to be good, though usually we weren't." He pondered that for a moment. "I've been discussing the necessity of education with Emma. We've been looking at some schools in the East, and we think we've come up with a few good choices she can apply to."

"Are you talking about boarding school for my daughter?" Taylor sounded horrified.

"Well, that sounds a bit harsh. I prefer finishing school. I mean, the definition is different, isn't it, but for my purposes, the term seems more appropriate."

Taylor shook her head. "Okay, helicopter dad. Hover all over your daughter if you want, but she's going to want to wear Ropers if the other girls are. She might even be a rodeo queen."

"Emma says she's going to be a nurse. She's planning on doing the extra schooling to become a nurse practitioner." Falcon nodded with satisfaction. "No military for my daughter, although her aunt Ash may protest. Ash thinks the military is a fine place for a young lady to learn real usable skills, but I—"

"Falcon," Taylor said, "you can't plan Emma's life for her."

"I'm not planning it. We discuss options, and she puts forth her opinion."

"How does she do that?" Taylor demanded. "When she's taking her bottle? Her nap?"

"Don't you worry, little mama," Falcon said confidently. "Emma and I discuss these things nightly. When we read our book and go to bed."

Taylor sighed and looked out as the young cowboys began to load up for the first event of bull riding. "Falcon, it's sweet that you want to protect Emma so much, but planning every second of her life isn't going to make her safer."

"It's better than planning nothing and letting something happen when she's four years old. Six years old. Fourteen." Darkness crossed his soul as he looked inward at the fear. "You don't understand that this might not ever be over. I don't know how long I'll be at Rancho Diablo, but at the moment, I'd say the chances of Emma graduating while I'm still riding fence there is pretty great."

He hadn't factored a child into his plans when he'd taken on this job. In fact, he hadn't figured in a woman, either, but this one sitting next to him was too sweet and sassy to ignore. Taylor had caught him the first time he'd laid eyes on her. It wasn't even about the ranch land he and his siblings were supposed to be battling for—though he'd love to win those twenty thousand acres north across the canyons.

But if he could just come out of this assignment with this woman as his wife, that would be win enough for him.

"I guess if you're going to send Emma off to a boarding school," Taylor said, "I'll go back to work, then."

He blinked. "Work? At Banger's?"

"Sure." She shrugged. "It's my job, right?"

"Well, yeah." He rubbed his chin. Men came into the diner, just like he had. Men sat at the bar and stared at Taylor, ogling her, just like he had.

He didn't want her ogled.

"There's no rush," he said, hedging as he stared into her eyes, sensing a trap might be getting laid for him. "Wouldn't you rather stay home with Emma for a while?"

"But Emma's going off to boarding school. And if I wait until you ship her off—what, at the age of three?—then my skills will be out of date."

"Six," he said automatically. "She'd probably start at six. They can in England, you know."

Taylor gasped. "Okay, Falcon. That's the final straw. You're not sending my daughter to England!"

"Some really awesome schools—"

She put up a hand. "I know what you're trying to do. You're trying to protect her. But you don't even want me working at Banger's. You're trying to protect yourself, Falcon Chacon Callahan. And control isn't the way to do it."

"That's because I fell for an opinionated woman," Falcon said. "Independent and feisty."

"That's right. So quit trying to send my child away from Rancho Diablo. This is where she belongs."

He flattened his mouth. "And if she gets stolen?"

"How would that happen? You never put her down!"

He grinned. "There's no reason to. In the tribe, babies are carried for quite some time."

"By the mother," Taylor said.

"But I'm very enlightened," Falcon said, still grinning, and Taylor sighed.

"Whatever. This is supposed to be a date. So let's date. Even though you're a little nutty, Falcon." She settled back against the bleachers, right where he could wrap his arm over her shoulders and give her a reassuring squeeze.

"Just a normal date night," he said, and Taylor said, "You and the adjective *normal* aren't used in the same sentence."

He laughed. Then his gaze caught something in the crowd, something he hadn't been expecting. He sat up, staring down into the arena, suddenly alert. "Do you see that barrel?"

Taylor sat up to get a better look. "Yes."

"Did you see the bullfighter who got in the barrel?"

"No." She glanced at him. "Did you know him?"

"Know him?" Falcon looked disgusted. "It's my brother."

"Brother?"

"Dante," he said. "That duty-shirking freak. Wait until I read him the riot act." Falcon couldn't believe it, but he would recognize his wily younger brother anywhere.

"Aren't they supposed to be doing PBR?"

"Yeah. Not these types of events." He shook his head. "I can't believe it. They left us shorthanded to jump out of barrels."

"It's an honorable living," Taylor said. "It's a great profession."

He looked at her with disgust. "We're trying to protect a ranch for our cousins. It's the mission we were assigned."

"Oh," Taylor said. "I guess that means you'll be doubly upset when I tell you that I believe I see Tighe over there sitting in the announcer's booth? He just finished running the mutton busting. I wasn't going to tell you, but…"

Falcon closed his eyes, sank back against the bleachers. "Worthless. Shiftless."

Taylor laughed. "It's not that bad, is it?"

"No," Falcon said. "At least it won't be if you'll agree to marry me."

She raised a brow. "Are you officially proposing?"

"Without all the trappings," he said sheepishly. "I don't have a ring. We'd have to stay here for a couple of days to do the proper paperwork, but I'd much rather be really spontaneous and fly to Vegas tonight."

"I…" Taylor looked confused. "You're proposing because your brothers have upset you?"

"I just don't want to be them. I like a plan, as you've noticed. I'm afraid if I don't get you to the altar, you'll slip away. You have all these opinions and a strong spirit," he said, very certain for the first time of what it was that had been making him so nervous about Taylor all this time. "You could change your mind about me, and then I'll be back to worrying about ol' Benton, and one day, I could end up in a barrel down there with Dante. I think you better tie me down as fast as you can, beautiful."

Chapter Seventeen

"On this paperwork," Taylor said, whispering in the Las Vegas chapel, "there's a question about your occupation. Can I put 'certifiable loon'?"

Falcon shook his head. "Put 'romantic devil.'"

"Oh, brother." Of course, the form hadn't included any such question, but Taylor couldn't resist the urge to tease her eager beau just a little. To try to knock some of the nervousness out of the man. She didn't really know what had gotten into Falcon, but the last few weeks since she'd been back, he'd been almost a different man than the one she'd made love to.

It was as if, ever since she'd been kidnapped, he had some kind of dark fear that he couldn't let go of. And it didn't matter if he was worrying about her or Emma, he just worried. "Are you sure you want to do this?"

"You're the mother of my child," he whispered back. "Of course I want to do this! I asked you once before, before you were the mother of my child, and I've asked you again now that we took the next step. Do I have to propose again after we have another baby? Reach the next stage in our relationship?"

She started to laugh at his reply, then realized he wasn't trying to be funny. "I guess not." She looked at him for a moment, her heart completely stolen by this big man. She couldn't imagine loving any other man the way she loved Falcon. And yet… "Falcon, you're making me nervous."

"All brides are nervous. I have this on good authority."

Taylor hesitated. Falcon had called the wedding chapel where they now stood for a drive-through wedding, which had sounded like a great lark to Taylor— at the time. He'd even booked the Elvis impersonator to croon for the ceremony. They'd gotten out of the car he'd rented at the airport, and were standing here, she in her blue jeans and him in his blue jeans, fresh from the rodeo, and… "Falcon," she whispered, "why didn't you go down to talk to Tighe and Dante?"

"I was too embarrassed. I was afraid I'd pop them one." He shook his head. "Sometimes it's better to hear no evil, see no evil, and then I do no evil."

"But why is what they were doing bad?"

"Because they deserted the family," he said simply. "Why are you worried about my brothers?"

"I'm not," she said slowly. "It's just that I think they're the reason you finally proposed." Elvis crooned away, and Taylor stood in the driveway, trying to gather her wits. "Falcon, I don't think you're in love with me."

His eyes widened. "Of course I'm in love with you. Have I not said that?"

"I—no."

"Huh." He frowned. "I guess I haven't. I guess I tell Emma I love you so often I thought I was saying it sometimes to you, too." He held her chin up and looked down into her eyes. "Taylor, I know you think I'm a little crazy—"

"Perhaps wired just a little differently."

"But I do love you. With all my heart. And I'm sorry about the ring, but I promise you will have something better than this thing I bought at the rodeo, one day."

She smiled. "I rather like it, actually."

"Are you going to marry me or not?" he said after a moment, when Elvis geared up for another song after Falcon waved a hand at him to keep going. "Because the thing that worries me the most—"

"Right now—"

"Right now," he said, "is that if we go back to Rancho Diablo and you haven't tied me down properly, I might lose you forever."

She smiled. Felt happiness spread all over her. "I will marry you, Falcon."

He got down on one knee, held her hand. "I love you, madly and passionately. You scare the hell out of me, too, but I like that about you. It's because you're stronger than me, and braver, too. And I'm taking on Diablo's best girl. You don't know how that can intimidate even a guy who considers himself pretty tough."

She laughed, pulled him to his feet. "Let's give Elvis a rest and say our I do's, cowboy."

"I thought you'd never ask."

"Here they come!" Fiona was so excited she could barely stand it, even if the wedding hadn't taken place at Rancho Diablo. She had Jillian and Taylor's mother, Mary, and her three dearest Books'n'Bingo Society friends, Corinne, Maxine and Taylor's aunt Nadine, with her. It hadn't been easy to wrap the ranch in beautiful wedding attire, with white and pink bows swirling from every corral post, and twinkling lights strung along the fences, before her nephew and his bride returned. Turning out a full guest list in time to welcome the newlyweds home was a far easier proposition—nobody wanted to miss a thing. There were gifts galore for Taylor and Falcon stacked in the big den.

Now all the guests were loaded up with rice and paper hearts to throw at the happy couple. "We're doing this a bit in reverse, but maybe it's good luck to throw the rice on them when they arrive instead of leave," Fiona murmured.

Nadine hovered nearby, stretching to try to see Falcon's truck rumbling up the drive. "Good thing they called to check on Emma, and alerted Ash to what they'd done."

"I didn't think they'd actually go through with it," Corinne said. "I almost thought we overdid it when Falcon came to ask our counsel."

"Overdid it?" Fiona glanced at her. "Not now, Corinne. We have a wedding to celebrate."

The rest of Falcon's siblings came over to stand next to her. "This is your big moment, Aunt Fiona," Galen teased.

"Believe me, I live for weddings. Don't think I don't. I should open my own matchmaking service."

Jace made a sound that was something like a snort. She stared at him suspiciously. "Were you going to say something, nephew?"

"No, aunt." Jace shook his head. "But some of us like you in the capacity in which you currently serve."

She didn't respond. She could read Jace's face. He was afraid he'd be up next, the scalawag, and maybe he would, now that Falcon was out of the way. Even if it was with an Elvis impersonator nearby, hardly a fit way to be married, when they should have been here at Rancho Diablo among friends, with the Diablos near, and Taylor wearing the magic wedding gown...

It would all work out. "Congratulations!" Fiona cried, and everybody tossed their rice and paper hearts as Falcon and Taylor got out of the truck and came to greet them. Taylor ran to hug her aunt Nadine, then wrapped Fiona in a warm embrace. Then Ash. "You told," she said to Falcon's sister.

"I forget Aunt Fiona goes a little overboard," Ash said.

"No, you didn't. What a lovely party. Thank you, Fiona," Taylor said.

"Yes, Aunt Fiona, thank you." Falcon hugged her, and Fiona felt her heart expand. This was her family; these were the reasons she'd immigrated from Ireland and stayed. Taking care of them, and gently managing them, had become her life's work.

Everyone greeted the newlyweds. Taylor brushed some rice from her hair after her braided rope ring had been duly admired, and glanced around. "Where's Emma?"

Fiona blinked. Whirled around. "Where's Emma?"

Jace, Galen, Sloan and Ash looked at each other.

"You had her last," Ash said to Sloan.

"I gave her to Galen. I had to put something up for Aunt Fiona," Sloan said.

"Jace held her for a moment so I could take a phone call about some horses for the ranch," Galen said.

"I put her in her crib when she got sleepy," Jace said. "That little port-a-crib we keep in the den."

Falcon took off running to the house. Taylor looked a little pale. "He's still going to be a very protective father," she said. "I'm shocked he wanted to go off for a night. He said the only reason he could do it was that he had four soldiers keeping their eyes on his daughter."

Falcon burst back outside. "Where's Emma? She's not in her crib."

Fiona's heart shriveled up with fear. She felt herself start to shake. Just a bit. Her heart thundered like the Diablo horses through the canyons. "I'm sure she's close by, Falcon. Everybody help us look!"

But Emma was nowhere on the ranch.

"I SHOULDN'T HAVE LEFT HER." Falcon loaded a gun, put another in his jeans. "I should have known that after Wolf took you, he'd take my child. I waited before, just like I was told by Grandfather, but I'm not waiting this time. I'm going to rain hellfire all over Wolf, and I don't care about Running Bear's rule about no killing. I'll take great pleasure in it."

"I'm going with you. Don't you dare try to leave me behind." Taylor grabbed two guns out of the concealed kitchen cabinet.

"I can't go through that again. You're staying," Falcon said, and Taylor put a hand on his arm to stop him from hurrying off.

"Falcon, either we're in this together or we're not. Your life is my life now, and vice versa. That means you don't keep me out of the bad times, and I don't tell you Emma doesn't go to finishing school. As much as I totally disagree with it."

He swallowed. "I don't like it. No man wants his wife in a—"

"It's okay," she interrupted. "We're going to do this together. Not only am I a good shot, I know his lair. Besides, Rosa and Ziha like me. I doubt very much they agree with what Wolf's done."

Falcon nodded. "All right. Come on. I'm going to book a pilot to take us to—"

"Wait," Taylor said. "That's what he expects you to do. He thinks you'll head to Montana because that's where I was before. He's not going there."

Falcon frowned. "We don't have a lot of time. We have to make the right choice now."

She took a deep breath. "I'd check the cave first. Wolf hasn't got the first idea how to deal with a baby. He has no children. Did he take the diaper bag?"

They looked around—no diaper bag. No baby carrier.

Falcon's brothers and sister trooped into the room, their expressions downcast. The guests had dispersed once they'd realized a dire emergency had arisen at Rancho Diablo.

"I'm so sorry," Ash said. "We'll help you look for her everywhere. Tell us what you want us to do."

Falcon stood still, frozen. Torn.

"First, someone call Sheriff Cartwright," Ash said. "Then we need to plan a thorough sweep through every inch of the canyons. Wolf's going to be expecting you, so you're going to have to sneak up on him. Don't you think that's the best course of action, Falcon?"

He roused himself from the fear gripping him. "Yes. I'll take the far side, nearest Storm Cash's place."

"I'll take the land nearest Bode Jenkins's property," Jace said.

"I'll take Xav's old post," Sloan said. "The farthest canyons."

"I'll take the middle," Ash said.

"I'm going to drive toward Diablo," Taylor said suddenly. "I've got a funny feeling we should check the main drag."

"Why?" they all asked.

Falcon looked at her, his gaze dark. "Why?"

He was listening to her, measuring her opinion. Their marriage would work out if they worked together instead of against each other—surely a terrible by-product of Wolf's plans if their marriage was destroyed.

She wouldn't let that happen.

"Because all the guests were here. Everybody was here. Our attention was distracted. He's not going to expect anybody to be in town right now. Nobody knows him except us. A man walking in with a baby is just going to look like another out-of-towner on his way through to Santa Fe. If I had a baby I didn't know what to do with, I might get her out of the heat and into a nice cool diner where I could sit and figure out what I was going to do with the little time bomb I'd snatched."

"If he has Ziha and Rose with him, he's got plenty of backup," Falcon pointed out.

She nodded. "They'll know a little bit about babies, but not much. They're mercenaries, not mothers." They hadn't seemed much like family people, either. Not many cooking skills, zero housekeeping skills. "Like I said, it's just a hunch I've got. The caves are more likely. But if I'd just grabbed a baby, I'd be thinking I'd better get to a grocery and stock up."

Falcon nodded. "I'll go with you."

"No. I could be wrong," Taylor said. "And besides, you're wearing enough firepower to scare the willies out of the town pillars."

"Everybody keep in touch by text," Falcon said,

"except for in the canyons. Be sure you have the new walkie-talkies. They'll get a good test today."

"We'll meet back here at dark," Taylor said, "and count heads. If anybody doesn't return, we'll come looking."

"Oh, dear," Fiona said. "I think I'll bake. Cook up a dinner. Come on, Burke. You can peel potatoes." She was shaking just a little, Taylor saw. Which meant she was completely rattled.

In all Fiona's years at Rancho Diablo, she'd never had one of her charges disappear—not a baby, anyway. Taylor felt sorry for her.

"It's going to be all right," she said, looking up at her big strong husband, who stared after his aunt and uncle with concern.

"I know. After I kill Wolf, it's going to be great. Let's go."

"Look," Falcon said, and Taylor leaned across him to peer out the window.

"Told you," she said. "I know my child, and her feeding schedule is not to be tinkered with by even fifteen seconds. Hang on."

She got out of the truck, and Falcon watched in shock as she strode across the grocery store parking lot and snatched Emma out of Wolf's arms, then slapped him hard across the face. Wolf stood rubbing his cheek, staring down at petite Taylor giving him the dressing-down of his life, every once in a while stepping back a little from her. Falcon got out of the truck, deciding after a quick moment that his wife seemed to have the entire situation under control.

As she'd said all along—she could handle this.

After a few moments, during which time Wolf seemed to be listening intently to everything Taylor said, his uncle slunk off. Taylor watched him go, waved to two women who were driving a truck Wolf got into, shook her finger at the henchman riding in the back, and then she walked back over to Falcon with their daughter in her arms.

"Whoa," he said. "I feel almost sorry for my dastardly uncle. Almost. Not quite."

He took his daughter in his arms. She gazed up at him, her deep blue eyes seeming to know everything, and he grinned back at her. "Emma says she was never worried. She says she knew we'd come for her."

Taylor leaned against his shoulder. "Your uncle says he's not going to give up. He said it wasn't his idea to take Emma—that was all Rhine's—and he was just on his way into the grocery story to buy diapers. He said he enjoyed getting to hold his great-niece, even if she did have a smelly situation going on."

"That's my girl," Falcon told Emma. "Doesn't let a thing bother her. She's going to be a tough spirit like her mother."

They got into the truck and strapped Emma into her car seat. "I wasn't really tough until I met you."

"I don't believe you. No one grows bravery skills in a day."

Taylor smiled, leaned over their daughter to kiss him on the lips. "You did," she said, and Falcon figured that was true. It had taken him months to finally get up the courage to ask Taylor to marry him, but when he finally had, there'd been no looking back. That night in the diner had changed everything.

"Come on, Emma," he said. "Let's go take you

home so we can let your aunts and uncles off the hook. They're suffering intense guilt."

"I feel so sorry for them," Taylor said. "You handled the whole thing much better than I thought you would, Falcon. I believe you're beginning to—"

"If you're going to say I'm starting to calm down about this dad thing, I wouldn't be too optimistic. I was about to have a heart attack. I wanted to yell my brothers' ears off, but I didn't have time." Falcon smiled a bit smugly. "It was enough to see them suffering."

"That's mean," Taylor murmured. "They love Emma. Anyway, it's not their fault. Wolf and Co. are sneaky."

"True."

"So, about finishing school for Emma," Taylor said, and Falcon said, "I'll probably send the applications off tomorrow."

Taylor shook her head and looked out the window, but she reached over to take his hand in hers, and he thought maybe she was trying not to laugh.

She had no idea that after he dropped her off at home, he had a small run to make to the canyons. Just a quick one. That's all the time he'd need, to set his uncle straight once and for all.

It was all about protecting his family. If Wolf wanted to talk to him so badly, he was going to get that opportunity.

Chapter Eighteen

"Uncle Wolf," Falcon said, striding into the cave without hesitation. It was dark outside, and the only light in the cave came from a fire and a couple of flashlights, but Falcon didn't need light. "Clear out."

"I'm not going anywhere," Wolf said.

"We'll see." Falcon glanced at the two women Taylor called Ziha and Rose, then studied Rhine. "I see your gun. If you so much as touch it, you won't be alive to eat breakfast in the morning. Just a friendly suggestion." He looked at his uncle, fury boiling inside him. "You took my daughter. You took my wife."

Wolf shrugged. "Opportunities present themselves."

"There'll be no more opportunities of any of the Callahan extended family tree."

"Can't make those promises," Wolf said. "You understand my position."

"I don't. If you're after our parents, we don't know what happened to them. Mom and Dad have been gone for years. We assume something happened to them on some job they were on. Our grandfather never said more than that. And our cousins' parents died long ago. So you're on a mission with no satisfactory conclusion."

"Wrong," Wolf said. He lit a cigarette. "Your parents

are in witness protection. We suspect the Callahans are, too. We never found graves or certificates of death, so—"

"Death certificates were filed for Molly and Jeremiah." Falcon frowned. "It doesn't matter. You took my daughter and my wife because you're determined to sink our family. It stops today. Or I discount Running Bear's instructions and I take you out."

Wolf smiled. "You'd be the one to do it, too. I know the risks."

"Who's backing you? Who hired you?" Falcon demanded.

"We're not going to talk about specifics today."

"We'll probably talk about specifics today," Galen said, walking into the cave, "because your troublemaking stops now, just like my brother told you."

"That's right," Ash said, coming to stand beside her brothers. "Turns out blood isn't that thick, after all. Not where you're concerned."

Sloan and Jace backed them up.

"How'd you know?" Falcon asked, and Ash shrugged.

"A little baby told us you'd gone out," she said.

"My wife and daughter," Falcon said, not surprised. "Okay, here's the deal," he told Wolf. "We've got nothing you want. Can't help you. Don't have control of Rancho Diablo. So you're wasting your time with our family. And our wives and children are completely off-limits to all of you, or we tie you to a cactus and leave you to wither away. Good times," Falcon said, looking over at Ziha and Rose. "For the record, my wife would disapprove of me discriminating against females. She's big on being a team player."

He thought they looked a bit pale, but wasn't sure. It

was so dim in the cave. "Take his gun, Ash," he said, pointing to Rhine, and she did.

"So. You're understanding me, uncle?"

Wolf spread his hands. "It's not right. The tribe backed the purchase of the land. The mineral rights are the tribe's. You don't have the right to get it all."

"Running Bear made those decisions. And why he chose to leave out his middle son, I don't know. I don't care." Falcon was hard-pressed not to let his anger fly, but figured it was a waste of energy. Wolf had his own reasons for what he did. "Tell me who put you up to all this. I know you're in deep with a cartel. You have to be, to sell out our family."

Wolf spread his hands again. "I'd be a dead man if I talked."

"You're probably a dead man, anyway," Falcon said. "It's them or us."

Wolf blinked. Hesitated.

And in that moment, Falcon knew the truth: Wolf wasn't in control of this battle. He couldn't stop it. He was just a minion. A greedy minion, true, who was willing to sell out his family to get what he considered his, but still, not the head honcho.

"All right." Falcon drew a deep breath. "Look at our faces. See us united. Know that we will protect our families. You've picked the wrong side of the war, but that's not our problem."

He walked out, and his siblings followed.

"It's not over," Galen said.

"True," Falcon said, "but now they know we'll take them on."

"I liked the part about the cactus," Ash said cheerfully. "That would be awesome!"

"How do we proceed from here?" Sloan asked.

"Yeah, what's the next step?" Jace wanted to know.

Falcon knew his uncle had been bottled only for the moment. There was too much at stake. Each side had too much to lose. And Wolf was guided by hatred for his brothers. Their uncle knew he'd been left behind by his own father, and that the spirit of the Diablos would never be under his control.

Unless he fought for it—hard.

They heard thunder in the canyons. The siblings looked toward the ring of fire and stone in the distance, and then they melted into the darkness.

"Now," Falcon said, as he met his wife in their bedroom, "where were we, about six months ago?"

Taylor smiled. "I believe we were sharing Christmas Eve in front of a fire. Which reminds me, I never got to give you your Christmas gift. Fiona saved it for me." She handed him the lone gift he'd seen under the tree.

"I don't have a Christmas present for you," Falcon said.

"Yes, you do." She winked at him, and he was certain he saw a sexy gleam in his wife's eyes. "But open that first."

He tore into the box, more interested in getting to kiss his wife than the gift. Lifting the lid, he dug around in the tissue, pulling out a tiny pair of blue baby booties. "Does Emma like blue?"

Taylor smiled. "They're for Emma's baby brother. When he makes his presence known, in a year or so."

Falcon swallowed. "You want another baby?"

"Well, it seems like you're handling this fathering thing pretty well—"

"Some days."

She leaned against him. He put the booties and box on the dresser so he had both hands free for his wife. Sighing, he wrapped her in his arms, holding her close. "You're determined to see this through?"

Taylor smiled. "What? Being married to you?"

"Yeah." He wondered sometimes. She definitely hadn't got the best end of the deal. Ol' Benton would have taken her fancy places, anywhere in the world, treated her like a princess. "I worry that Jillian was right. She said you'd be marrying down if you married me, and I guess you did."

Taylor looked up at him. "Maybe."

He gulped, worried.

"But then again, I never really agreed with Jillian's assessment. I was so afraid you wouldn't wait until December for me."

"December?" He shook his head. "I ended up waiting until June for you. I would have been thrilled to marry you in December."

Sudden banging on the door downstairs stopped what he was saying. "Hold on to that thought. It was going someplace."

He went downstairs, Taylor following him. Opening the door, he found Storm Cash on the other side. "Evening, Storm."

Storm nodded. "Do you have a moment?"

Falcon glanced at Taylor. "I guess. What's up?"

"Remember when I told you I'd found evidence of squatters on my land?"

"Yes."

"I caught them. Bring them up, Sheriff."

Sheriff Cartwright brought Ziha and Rose to the

door. Falcon looked at Taylor, who appeared vaguely worried.

"They claim they know you, Callahan. I doubt their story, though. Why would they camp on my land if they're friends of yours?"

Falcon sighed. "They're not friends of ours."

"But do you know them?"

"What's going on?" Fiona came to the door in her robe, with Burke not far behind her.

"And this guy, too," one of the deputies said. He shoved Wolf toward the door. "He claims he's your uncle, Falcon."

Well, this was not good. His sister and brothers came to join him, standing around staring silently at the people on the porch.

"Hi, kids," Wolf said. "Long time no see."

"This is what you get for not tying him to the cactus when you had the chance," Taylor whispered. She had Emma in her arms now, comforting her.

Falcon wondered if he was ever going to have one minute alone with his wife. "Where'd you find them, Storm?"

"Camping out in the open."

Why would Wolf have moved from the cave to the open?

So he'd get caught. And get to lay claim to the Callahan family, officially.

Falcon looked his uncle in the eye. "Never saw him before in my life, Sheriff." He closed the door. "Nothing more to see here, folks. Move along. Everyone back to bed."

"Wait a minute," Ash said. "What's Wolf up to?"

"His next ploy is to move right on into the family."

Falcon shrugged, looked at Galen. "He's tried to get what he wants in an underhanded manner, now he's going into the open. Where we have to acknowledge him. Next thing we know, he'll be spreading rumors about us around town. Mouthing off to everyone about how poorly we treat our family relations."

Taylor kissed Emma on the head. "I feel sorry for Ziha and Rose."

"See?" He looked at his family. "That's how it starts. Playing us against each other. We can't afford to let him."

"I agree with Falcon," Ash said. "We have no reason whatsoever to take that genie out of the bottle."

For some reason, they all looked at Taylor. She looked back at them. "What?"

"You know them better than any of us," Ash said. "Do you have any input?"

Taylor blinked. "I don't know them. They're not my family. I…"

She stopped, confused. Wolf was connected to her, since he was Falcon's uncle. And she had lived with them, in the enemy's lair, so to speak. "I don't really know anything about Wolf. I didn't see him that much. They didn't seem all that cohesive. Rhine appears to do the dirty work. The girls are for protection, I think. I don't think they like Wolf very much. And your uncle—" She shrugged. "He keeps to himself mostly. They'll eat anything, that's the best I can tell you."

But it bothered her that they'd asked. She didn't know why, but it did. Maybe she'd never seen herself as some kind of double agent. Or worse, that she'd been there willingly. Was that what Falcon was asking her?

"Your grandfather told me not to try to leave," Taylor

told Falcon. "He said the winter and spring were long, that before the real thaw tempers would fray, and then would be my chance." She looked at her husband. "I didn't want to be there."

"I know you didn't." He looked surprised. "Believe me, none of us wanted you to be there."

She nodded. "Okay. I'm going back to the nursery with Emma."

Falcon followed. "Taylor, I didn't mean that how it sounded. I didn't mean that you were happy being there."

"I know." She put Emma in her crib. "Don't you think you should be honest with the sheriff? Tell him that Wolf is your uncle and that he's been causing all kinds of problems for your family?"

"I don't know." Falcon sank into the rocker, watching her as she rubbed Emma's back. "My instinct is to keep Wolf completely out of our lives."

She turned away. "You know better than me."

He went to her, reaching out to draw her to him. "Taylor, those months you were gone, it killed me that I couldn't go get you. I felt like the world's biggest heel. I relied on Running Bear to know the best way to play his son. But it was hard as hell. And I am sorry." He kissed the top of her head. "I just don't want him anywhere near you or Emma ever again, and I'll deny his existence up and down and in the face of angels if I have to. For me, he just doesn't exist. He's a black force I'm going to fight, but he's not my uncle and he's got no claim on Rancho Diablo."

She nodded. "I know."

"Or on our marriage. I love you, Taylor."

She smiled, feeling as if all the clouds suddenly lifted. "I love you, too, Falcon."

"Let me tell you a bedtime story, since Emma sacked out," Falcon said, and Taylor pulled him down the hall to pick up where they'd left off so many months ago.

FALCON WOKE UP EARLY, kissed his sleeping wife with a tender smile. He would have dearly loved to awaken her for another sweet reunion, but he had to be satisfied that finally he had her back in his arms.

It had been too long.

Making love to her had been even more amazing than before, maybe because of everything they'd been through, or maybe because now she was his wife. Forever.

"I was just meant to be married," he told his daughter, who was lying awake in her crib, playing happily with her toes. "You're such a good girl. Why are you always so sweet? You get that from your mother's side of the family, for certain." He carried her down the hall and down the stairs, heading into the kitchen to warm up a bottle and read the paper with his tiny angel.

To his surprise, there was a knock on the front door. Since people they knew usually used the kitchen door, he wondered who would knock at this hour.

He opened it to find Sheriff Cartwright. "Good morning, Sheriff."

The big man nodded. "I'm here on official business, I'm afraid."

"Oh?"

"I need to speak to your wife, Falcon."

He didn't like the sound of that. "What's up, Sheriff?"

"According to Mr. Wolf Chacon, whom we kept overnight on the trespassing inquiry, you do know him. And your wife stayed with him recently for a few months. Is that true?"

Falcon sighed. "All you need to know about Wolf Chacon is that he's a criminal."

"Who is it, Falcon?" Taylor came to stand behind him. Then he realized his siblings and Fiona and Burke were around her. She took Emma from him. "Good morning, Sheriff."

He nodded. "Good morning, Callahans."

"Come into the kitchen, Sheriff," Fiona said. "I've got gingerbread on, and some hot coffee."

"Official business, Fiona." He looked at Taylor. "If I could have a moment of your time, please."

She looked at Falcon. His heart felt like a stone inside him. How he wished he could protect her from this. But this was why Jillian had warned Taylor away from him, away from the Callahans.

He shrugged. She was going to have to make her own decisions about what she wanted to reveal. She was the one who'd been taken as a hostage; he wasn't about to tell her how to address questions about that. It was her life. He just wanted to be in her life.

"Go right ahead, Sheriff," Taylor said.

"The land where Wolf and his companions were found was on the border between yours and Mr. Cash's. Storm Cash is of a mind to press charges. He says he's had all kinds of trouble with trespassers. But Mr. Chacon claims that he's a Callahan, and therefore, not guilty of anything more than stepping onto a neighbor's property accidentally in the darkness. He says you can vouch for him, Mrs. Callahan." The sheriff glanced at

Falcon. Ash and his brothers ringed Taylor protectively, but he hung back, not wanting to get in the way of whatever decision she made.

"I did stay with Wolf Chacon for a while," Taylor said. "And I wasn't happy about it. He and his people took me from this house and kept me in Montana with them. I doubt that's the story Wolf wants me to tell you, Sheriff. I'm sure he thinks I'll repeat Falcon's story, or that I'll be too intimidated to tell the truth. But that's the real truth. He's an evil man, and the best thing that could happen," she said, with an apologetic look at Falcon, "is locking him up for a long time."

It was as if a long breath exhaled from the entire Callahan clan, including Fiona. They all stared at Falcon, wondering what he'd say. He thought his wife's speech had been a pretty good one.

Sheriff Cartwright looked at all the Callahans. "So he's telling the truth when Mr. Chacon says he's your uncle?"

"Not one we officially recognize," Falcon said. "Kind of the crazy uncle you hope never shows up in your life. He has, and we're dealing with it."

"I see." The sheriff rocked back on his heels for a moment, thinking. "Troublemaker, is he?"

"Mildly," Falcon said. They weren't breaking his grandfather's rules. Running Bear had said they couldn't kill him—but he'd never said they couldn't hand him over to the authorities. And Falcon and his siblings hadn't done it, anyway. Taylor had. She was outside the rules, as he saw it.

This was going very smoothly.

And if it kept going this smoothly, surely he'd get his happy ending. He'd know he wasn't the hunted one his grandfather warned of, the one who was foretold to bring great trouble to the family. Great sacrifice. A division, unless the hunted one resisted the darkness.

"I see," Sheriff Cartwright said. "Didn't you tell me last night that you'd never seen him before in your life, Falcon?"

Falcon nodded. "I did."

"I'm sure you know that falls under the heading of hindering an investigation. And aiding and abetting a criminal, since none of you revealed that he's been on your land, and in your home. Hindering an investigation is against the law," Sheriff Cartwright said sternly.

"I'm sorry, Sheriff. I'm doing what I can to protect my family."

The lawman's lips flattened. "I'm afraid you're going to have to come down to the station with me, Falcon. I'm going to have to place you under arrest, much as I hate to do it."

"No!" Taylor looked stunned. "Sheriff Cartwright, please. If you only knew what trouble Wolf and his people have caused this family—"

"I know. I know. The Callahans have been fighting the good fight for a long time. I try to be a help as much as I can. I always have. Even when Jonas and his crew were always fighting with Bode Jenkins and the mercenary that made their life miserable back then. That Sonny character." He shook his head. "But the law's the law, and Jonas never lied to me outright. That's hindrance I can't overlook, Falcon." He looked at their aunt, who was stubbornly standing with her arms crossed. "I'm sorry, Fiona. I wish I could help, but the law's the law."

"Well, this is a fine situation," Fiona said. "I guess

you can put Falcon in a cell next to Wolf and they can play tiddledywinks. Or cards."

"Sheriff, please." Taylor's face was pale. "Falcon didn't want to say that I'd been kidnapped. I haven't wanted all of Diablo to know that. You know my family, you know I've always been something of a—"

"Daughter of the town," Sheriff Cartwright said. "I know, Taylor. I love you like a daughter, too. You're one of our best girls."

"I wanted everyone to think I was just traveling with Mom," Taylor insisted. "My way of dealing with what happened was just to forget that it had. I don't want to be seen as a victim, Sheriff. And I don't want you to take my husband off to jail."

"I'm going," Falcon said. "It's going to be all right. If you can handle five months in Montana, I can handle some time in jail. Galen, bond me out fast, okay? I've got an errand to run." He went off with the sheriff and his deputy before things could get any more out of whack. Taylor looked as if she was going to cry—and that was the first time he'd ever seen his wife close to anything resembling tears. He felt quite helpless.

"Can I send a lunch sack with him, Sheriff, at least?" Fiona called after them. "And maybe something for the station, as well? I'm sure you'd like a little breakfast, too."

The sheriff shook his head ruefully, then helped Falcon into the car. "Thanks, Fiona. Another time."

They left, and Taylor stared at the squad car as it pulled away. She was vaguely aware of Fiona and Ash patting her, trying to comfort her. But she couldn't be comforted. The last thing she'd wanted was to hurt Falcon. Why hadn't she kept her mouth shut?

"It's okay," Ash said. "You did the right thing, Taylor."

"I did?" She couldn't understand how Falcon was ever going to forgive her. She hadn't done the right thing for him. "Oh, Emma," she murmured. "Your daddy isn't going to like me very much."

"Pfft," Fiona said. "If you think that a morning in jail is going to affect Falcon's feelings for you, you don't know him very well. It's all in a day's work around here, just part of the battle. We deal with it."

"That's right," Galen said. "Falcon's been in much worse places than a jail cell in Diablo."

"Yeah," Jace said. "The sheriff'll probably let him out on his own reconnaissance before we can get down there to do it."

Sloan sighed. "As long as he knows you and Emma are safe, Falcon won't care about anything."

Ash shrugged. "It's wacky. We take it one step at a time. But it's no fairy tale, so don't look for a happy ending. Not yet, anyway." She followed Fiona down the hall.

"Thanks, guys." Taylor looked at Emma, then after the people who were filing into the kitchen to discuss the next step and grab some breakfast. She kissed Emma's downy head, feeling awful that after a wonderful night of lovemaking, she'd sent her husband to jail.

This was bad. She wondered if Falcon could forgive her for this. But she had no intention of letting Wolf destroy their marriage. They'd barely found each other again, and she wasn't letting Falcon go now.

"We have a few choices, Emma. We can ignore the situation, see what happens. It's a bit above our pay grade, this mercenary thing, and we're obviously not all that helpful. Two, we can go home to Mom's place for a while, let the smoke clear, think about whether we're deadweight on your daddy or not. You'd like staying with Grandma, and I'd like pretending for just a moment that it was a standard visit, but it feels kind of cowardly and I'd miss your daddy too much. Three, we can head down to the jail and make sure your father gets sprung with all due haste."

Emma let out a squawk and waved a fist. "That's exactly what I thought," Taylor said. "Let's go raise a bit of Callahan heck. You might as well start young."

TAYLOR HAD EVERY intention of telling Falcon how sorry she was, and how she had to tell the truth—though the truth hadn't exactly set them free this time, so there was probably a learning curve involved. But when she got down to Sheriff's Cartwright's small jail in Diablo, she heard laughter and general male shenanigans going on. She walked in carefully with Emma, looking for Falcon.

He was perched on the edge of Sheriff Cartwright's desk. The two of them were playing a card game with two deputies. Wolf and his stooges were nowhere to be found. "Is this how jails are run nowadays?" Taylor asked, walking over to the men.

"Are you here to spring your husband, Taylor?" Sheriff Cartwright asked.

"I didn't bring a file in a cake or anything, if that's what you're asking," Taylor said, and for some reason, all the men thought that was quite hilarious.

She didn't think it was funny at all. "What's going on? Where's Wolf?"

"Who?" Sheriff Cartwright glanced around the

room, looked at his deputies. "Anybody here by that name?"

They all laughed again. Taylor felt as if she was in the Diablo version of a frat house. She looked at her husband. "What's going on?"

"I was waiting on you to give me a ride home." He stood, tossed down his cards. "Sheriff, you beat me again."

"You'll improve in time. Goodbye, Falcon. Miss Emma, it's always a pleasure," Sheriff Cartwright said, kissing the baby's tiny fist. Emma's blue eyes laughed, and then she reached for her father, who took her in his big arms.

"Gentlemen, always an honor. Come on, wife. I have an errand to run. Not another day's going to go by until I get it done, either."

He waved to the sheriff and his men, then put his arm around Taylor, and they walked out into the warm Diablo day that was already heating up nicely.

"Do you mind telling me what's going on?" Taylor demanded. "What was all that back there?"

Falcon laughed. "Just making sure we kept Wolf on the straight and narrow. It's important for him to know that his cover's blown, and the law is looking for him now, too. Anytime he shows his face, he's a marked man. Sheriff Cartwright let him off with a warning to get out of town this time, but next time, it'll be all-out war on him and his cadre of thieves."

"You're not upset with me?"

He laughed. "I'm upset with you, darling. I'm so upset with you I'm about to replace that rope ring on your finger with the prettiest ring you can find in Diablo's jewelry store. Let's go pick something out for you, and then something for my angel, too." He kissed Emma's head. "I'm kind of partial to those silver baby bracelets. What do you think, wife?"

Taylor shook her head. "That you're crazy, mainly. I don't understand what happened—"

"You want an explanation or a wedding ring right now?" Falcon asked, kissing her on the lips.

"I really, really want to know what happened, Falcon," Taylor said. "I was just so certain I'd done the wrong thing by telling the truth."

"Nope," he said, kissing her again, "you did the right thing. You're always going to do the right thing. I love you, Taylor. I love your honesty and your spirit and your bravery. Once the sheriff knew that Wolf had been stalking you and Emma, he sent his deputies to take him and his people to some faraway canyon he's never heard of. It'll take him a good while to get back here." Falcon touched her hair, lingering. "And you did what none of us could—you turned our uncle in. He'll always be around making trouble, but this time, his plans backfired on him big-time, thanks to you. Only you could do what needed to be done, because of the legend. How awesome is your mother?" he asked Emma, holding his baby up in the air.

Taylor glanced around, seeing faces pressed up against the windows of Diablo's stores, smiling at them. Occasionally someone waved at her. She saw Jillian shoot her an okay sign from Banger's Bait and Tackle diner entry. When Falcon pulled her into his arms for another kiss, Taylor thought she heard applause from several of the shops.

Maybe it wasn't the way she'd ever thought her life would turn out. It was so much better than she could have ever dreamed. And the best part was, there was no place she'd rather be but right here in Diablo with her Callahan man and her daughter.

"About those blue booties," she told Falcon, and he winked at her.

"This time, the ring first, Taylor Callahan, and then you can fill up all the baby booties you want. Emma wants lots of siblings. She told me she did."

They kissed their daughter, and then they started walking down the main street of Diablo, a family forever.

And if they heard thunder in the distance on a perfectly beautiful clear sunny day, who was to say it wasn't the Diablos running wild and free, their spirits forever untamed.

Epilogue

"It's tradition," Fiona told her, and Ash laughed as she helped Taylor put the beautiful veil on. "All the Callahan brides get married twice. Besides, an Elvis impersonator isn't really right for a wedding, is it? I'm positive Emma would like to see photos one day of her parents getting married traditionally."

"Besides, Aunt Fiona just loves weddings. If you hadn't heard that already." Ash smiled at her. "You look beautiful, Taylor. And I sneaked a peek at your new wedding ring. Much better than that rope thing."

"I kind of liked the rope ring," Taylor murmured.

"I kind of like the sparkly solitaire heart my brother got you. It's about time he forked out. I was afraid I was going to have to talk to him, lead him through the steps of romance he was clearly missing. One last finishing touch," Ash said, putting the final pin in, and then she and Fiona surveyed their handiwork.

"Gorgeous," Fiona said. "Falcon's going to sweep you away and we may not see you for a week."

"Thank you." Taylor could almost feel magic in the air, a sense of wonder that she, too, was joining the brides of Rancho Diablo. From the upstairs window, she could see guests milling about on the grounds, enjoying the decorations Fiona and her friends had created. The Callahans had come home from Dark Diablo and Hell's Colony to celebrate, and the homecoming was joyful and sentimental for everyone. Taylor knew how much work and sacrifice everyone was making to protect this land, this ranch, and everything for which it stood.

"Ready?" Ash asked. "It's time to put on the magic wedding dress."

Taylor stood, smiling. She'd insisted that the short veil she'd chosen be put on first, then the wedding gown. The legend couldn't possibly be true, of course. Fairy tales were just that. Supposedly, all the Callahan brides had worn the magic wedding gown, and all had seen their true love's face. Which wasn't practical, of course. Just as Ash claimed to not believe in destiny, Taylor had never believed in ghosts, though her husband's family seemed very inclined to believe in ghosts and spirits and all manner of ancient lore. But no dress could conjure magic.

She'd insisted she put that on last so they wouldn't be disappointed when nothing special happened. She didn't know if she was a good enough storyteller to claim that she saw twinkles of stardust or a bolt of luminous lightning or whatever it was that supposedly accompanied the Callahans' romantic visions.

Ash and Fiona helped Taylor step into the dress.

"Close your eyes," Fiona told her.

"And click my heels three times?" Taylor teased.

"Whatever helps you focus," Ash said.

Taylor giggled, excited to see herself in the gown. "Can I open them?"

"Not until I have you all buttoned up. This gown transitions to every bride with its own special magic for her hopes and dreams," Fiona said, "and I never mess with magic. I follow all recipes with infinite devotion, and this dress is no different."

Taylor couldn't wait to see the gown. She felt Fiona and Ash step away from her, murmur how stunning, how fitting, how perfect.

Then she didn't hear any more.

"Can I open my eyes?"

No answer. Taylor opened her eyes, turned around to look for Ash and Fiona. To her surprise, Falcon stood there.

Her heart leaped with joy. "You're not supposed to see the bride before the wedding. Isn't it supposed to be bad luck?" Taylor asked, laughing. "Of course, we're already married, so it doesn't matter. Not that I believe in silly superstitions, anyway."

He smiled, his navy eyes admiring, absolutely the most handsome man she'd ever seen, the man who'd held her heart for so long she couldn't remember when he'd first won it—and then he disappeared.

Taylor gasped, then looked down at the stunning gown in wonder. She touched the tiny crystals and sequins with a joyous smile, then went down the stairs, feeling every inch a Callahan bride.

FALCON'S HEART NEARLY stopped when he saw Taylor at the top of the white runner that had been laid down the aisle between the white chairs filled with guests and family. Fiona held Emma, who wore her new baby bracelet and a white, lacy gown and tiny white lace booties, in a front row seat. Burke sat next to them, proudly keeping his wife company.

The music began. As maid of honor, Ash walked

first, grinning at Falcon because she knew very well he only had eyes for his wife. Taylor came down the aisle on Galen's arm, and the world felt perfect to him. Oh, the danger wasn't over, and the legend still had to come to pass. The hunted one would rise or fall according to events they couldn't control.

But in this one moment, everything was perfect.

"You've made me the happiest man in the world," he told her as she reached his side.

"Sweetie, we're already married," she whispered back, smiling.

"It doesn't matter. Feels like the first time all over again. I love you."

She smiled at him, and his world fell into place. "I got Diablo's best girl," he said, bragging just a bit, and his words accidentally got picked up by the deacon's microphone so that all the guests heard, and applause broke out, and happy laughter.

He kissed Taylor, even though the service hadn't yet started. The guests applauded again, and he told himself he had to quit or they were never going to get the marriage ceremony started. Taylor touched his arm, and he looked past the deacon into the distance, where Running Bear sat astride a Diablo, watching the ceremony. Falcon took Emma from his aunt Fiona and held his two best girls close, and Running Bear waved, before riding away, the sound of hooves echoing as he disappeared into the canyons.

But the hoofbeats became louder, and Falcon knew it was the sound of Diablos running, too, a reminder of all that the Callahans loved and stood for. Now he had Taylor and Emma, and the blessings were mystical, magical, just as he'd always imagined love could be, if he could find the right woman.

And he had.

They stood arm in arm, and he held Emma as the deacon intoned the marriage ceremony, and the sun shone gently over Rancho Diablo, ever so much like heaven on earth.

Falcon had found his heart, his home, his heaven, and she was standing right next to him, even though he'd never quite believed this could happen for him.

It had. Which just proved that good guys did indeed win the girl, with the help of family and friends and maybe, just maybe, a little bit of magic.

* * * * *

Watch for Dante's story,
BRANDED BY A CALLAHAN,
coming July 2013,
onlyfrom Harlequin American Romance

REQUEST YOUR FREE BOOKS!
2 FREE NOVELS PLUS 2 *FREE GIFTS!*

H HARLEQUIN®

American Romance®

LOVE, HOME & HAPPINESS

YES! Please send me 2 FREE Harlequin® American Romance® novels and my 2 FREE gifts (gifts are worth about $10). After receiving them, if I don't wish to receive any more books, I can return the shipping statement marked "cancel." If I don't cancel, I will receive 4 brand-new novels every month and be billed just $4.49 per book in the U.S. or $5.24 per book in Canada. That's a savings of at least 14% off the cover price! It's quite a bargain! Shipping and handling is just 50¢ per book in the U.S. and 75¢ per book in Canada.* I understand that accepting the 2 free books and gifts places me under no obligation to buy anything. I can always return a shipment and cancel at any time. Even if I never buy another book, the two free books and gifts are mine to keep forever.

154/354 HDN FVPK

Name	(PLEASE PRINT)	
Address		Apt. #
City	State/Prov.	Zip/Postal Code

Signature (if under 18, a parent or guardian must sign)

Mail to the Harlequin® Reader Service:
IN U.S.A.: P.O. Box 1867, Buffalo, NY 14240-1867
IN CANADA: P.O. Box 609, Fort Erie, Ontario L2A 5X3

**Want to try two free books from another line?
Call 1-800-873-8635 or visit www.ReaderService.com.**

* Terms and prices subject to change without notice. Prices do not include applicable taxes. Sales tax applicable in N.Y. Canadian residents will be charged applicable taxes. Offer not valid in Quebec. This offer is limited to one order per household. Not valid for current subscribers to Harlequin American Romance books. All orders subject to credit approval. Credit or debit balances in a customer's account(s) may be offset by any other outstanding balance owed by or to the customer. Please allow 4 to 6 weeks for delivery. Offer available while quantities last.

Your Privacy—The Harlequin® Reader Service is committed to protecting your privacy. Our Privacy Policy is available online at www.ReaderService.com or upon request from the Harlequin Reader Service.

We make a portion of our mailing list available to reputable third parties that offer products we believe may interest you. If you prefer that we not exchange your name with third parties, or if you wish to clarify or modify your communication preferences, please visit us at www.ReaderService.com/consumerschoice or write to us at Harlequin Reader Service Preference Service, P.O. Box 9062, Buffalo, NY 14269. Include your complete name and address.

HARI3

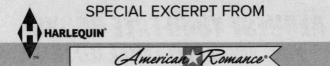
The Texas Lawman's Woman

by Cathy Gillen Thacker

Welcome to Laramie County, Texas, where you're bound to run into the first man you ever loved....

Shelley Meyerson's heart leaped as she caught sight of the broad-shouldered lawman walking out of the dressing room. She blinked, so shocked she nearly fell off the pedestal. "*He's* the best man?"

Colt McCabe locked eyes with Shelley, looking about as pleased as Shelley felt. His chiseled jaw clenched. "Don't tell me *she's* the maid of honor!"

"Now, now, you two," their mutual friend, wedding planner Patricia Wilson, scolded, checking out the fit of Shelley's yellow silk bridesmaid dress. "Surely you can get along for a few days. After all, you're going to have to…since you're both living in Laramie County again."

Don't remind me, Shelley thought with a dramatic sigh.

Looking as handsome as ever in a black tuxedo and pleated white shirt, Colt sized Shelley up. "She's never going to forgive me."

For good reason, Shelley mused, remembering the hurt and humiliation she had suffered as if it were yesterday. She whirled toward Colt so quickly the seamstress stabbed her with a pin. But the pain in her ribs was nothing compared to the pain in her heart. She lifted up her skirt, revealing her favorite pair of cranberry-red cowgirl boots, and stomped off the pedestal, not stopping until they were toe to toe. "You stood me up on prom night, you big galoot!"

Lips thinning, the big, strapping lawman rocked forward on the toes of his boots. "I got there."

Yes, he certainly had, Shelley thought. And even that had been the stuff of Laramie, Texas, legend. The town had talked about it for weeks and weeks. "Two hours late. Unshowered. Unshaven." Shelley threw up her hands in exasperation. "No flowers. No tuxedo…."

Because if he had looked then the way he looked now… Well, who knew what would have happened?

Read more of *THE TEXAS LAWMAN'S WOMAN*
this May 2013, and watch for the rest of this
new miniseries McCABE HOMECOMING
by Cathy Gillen Thacker.
Only from Harlequin® American Romance®!

HAREXPO513

HARLEQUIN®

American ★ Romance®

This cowboy has got trouble written all over him... How can she resist?

Forget cowboys! Ever since she was a girl, India Pike has had an image of the perfect man: sophisticated, refined and with a preference for tailored suits. But after rodeo promoter Liam Parrish came to town, she can't stop mooning over the gorgeous cowboy and single dad. Too bad Liam's totally wrong for her...even if the town's matchmaker already has India saying "I do."

Her Perfect Cowboy

by TRISH MILBURN

**Available April 23 from
Harlequin® American Romance®.**

Available wherever books are sold.